PRISM

FAYE KELLERMAN

PRISM

ALIZA KELLERMAN

HARPER
An Imprint of HarperCollins*Publishers*

Library of Congress Cataloging-in-Publication Data is available.
ISBN 978-0-06-168721-1 (trade bdg.) — ISBN 978-0-06-168722-8 (lib. bdg.)

Typography by Andrea Vandergrift
09 10 11 12 13   LP/RRDB   10 9 8 7 6 5 4 3 2 1
❖

To the Biloon family:
Ron, Jeremy, Ruthie, and Marcia—alehah Hashalom.
May her spirit be in a better universe.
—F.K.

To my parents, my friends, and my siblings—
the best friends of all.
—A.K.

Special thanks to Carrie Feron for starting the process.
A very special thanks to Rosemary Brosnan,
whose help and guidance were invaluable.
—F.K. & A.K.

1

I always half-believed that Fridays could make me fly. On days like this—with the air as crisp as a potato chip and the sky as clear as crystal—I felt featherlight as the three o'clock bell rang out, the most liberating sound on the planet. With my messenger bag strapped over my shoulder, I held my arms straight out at my sides and twirled like an Olympic skater, shrieking, "Thank God!"

"Say it again, sweets," Maria chimed in.

"Thank!" I roared, "God!"

She pulled one of my braids—a ratty purple thing—and her expression turned indecipherable. "Quick! Name five things more stupid than our upcoming class trip next week!"

I tapped my shoe on the ground and looked back at the clean outline of Buchanan High School. "Male models, neo-punk music, buttered-popcorn-flavored jelly beans, and the outfit I'm currently wearing."

"That's only four!" she chirped as we walked leisurely away from school.

"Okay! Okay, let's see—"

"How about Zeke Anderson? He's pretty stupid." Maria was the only girl—the only person—I knew who could tuck her shirt into her pants and wear suspenders ironically. She had recently hacked off her own hair, perhaps in a manic fit.

I'm kidding, though. Maria's not *really* manic.

"Ah, the Zekester," I said in a deep, jock voice. I then contorted my hand into the "rock on" symbol.

"No, Kaida!" Maria was disapproving. "Swimmies don't say rock on. They go like this."

She pulled out her hand to give me a high five and I smacked mine into her palm. I said, "Speaking of Monsieur Anderson, guess who's in my van for the class trip?"

"No!" she squealed, and pushed on the bag on my back.

I stumbled forward. "Maria!"

"Just kidding. Is Zeke really in your van?"

"Would I lie about this?" I was muttering to myself. "He's so . . ."

The word I was looking for was *ridiculous*. Zeke Anderson was nothing but ridiculous. He was overachieving to the point of annoyance, the stereotypical high-school queen bee, except for the addition of a Y chromosome. And next Wednesday, starting at nine in the morning, I'd be stuck with him and the constant witticisms emanating from his wide, white-toothed grin for hours on end. Zeke Anderson: proof positive that a person can be too perfect.

Growl.

"Dreamy!" Maria crooned in falsetto.

"Who's in your van?" I had hopes of her being grouped with someone as equally hilarious as Zeke.

She hesitated and gave me the pity smile. "Both Stephen and Iggy are in my van."

"What!" I exclaimed. She patted my head and I swatted her hand away. "You got Stephen . . . *Stephen*!" I was growling again. "And you got Iggy? How'd you get *both* of them?"

"The good fairy must like me."

"Meaning the good fairy hates me? What'd I do to her to merit Zeke Anderson?"

"There are worse things than Zeke the Geek." Maria squeezed my hand. "Come on. Who else is in your van? You had to get a few okay people."

"The only other person is Tallon." I pulled a pack of M&Ms out of my skirt. I love skirts with pockets.

"Tallon . . . Tallon . . . As in Joy Tallon? You mean she's the *only* other person in your van?"

"Yes, and yes. Why? How many people are in your van?"

"Like twelve. I guess there were an odd number of students

and that's why you have the small van. Well, cheer up, sugar. Joy's kind of nice. Her only vice is that her breath is awful."

"That's because she smokes like three packs a day." Joy Tallon was smart. But it was the kind of intelligence that leads to boredom, isolation, and eventually sadness. She was fourteen and a sophomore. She was also pretty, but faded pretty, like her edges had been rubbed away. It just made her all the more tragic.

"How do you think the trip will be?" Maria clearly wanted to change the conversation for my benefit.

"Maria," I said skeptically.

"Yes, Kaida?" she replied with the innocence of a sockhopper.

"Maria, dear. Darling. My best friend in this whole universe. We have been discussing this all month! This trip is going to be awful. It's going to suck. It will *not* be"—I cleared my throat and spoke an octave lower, to mimic Principal Warwick—"an educational experience that will broaden horizons."

Maria stared into the distance as we passed the local grocery store. We were about ten minutes from our houses. "I never did understand that figure of speech. You know, broaden your horizon. Isn't everyone's horizon more or less the same? How do you broaden it? By looking through 3-D glasses?"

I shrugged. "Maybe a horizon in the Serengeti is different from a horizon in the city." I thought about that. "I need to go to the drugstore. I want to pick up some Benadryl before the trip."

"Benadryl?"

"You know, in case there's pollen or a dog or something."

"Sure."

We walked a few minutes in silence, enjoying the freedom that only a weekend can bring. Although Maria and I lived just an hour away from the lights and glam of Hollyweird, California, St. Denis could have been Anywhere, USA—a combination of old-town charm and ugly strip malls. Today we chose the old-town route where cars still parked on the diagonal. The stores that lined the avenue were one story and faced with brick. Not *made* of brick because St. Denis was still on the California fault line and subject to earthquakes.

When we entered the Olde Chemist Shoppe—better known as a drugstore—a little bell sang out.

Maria snarled in an attempt to be frightening. "If I were you, I wouldn't be worried about a stupid dog causing you allergies. I'd be worried about the *bats*. I've heard they carry *rabies*."

"*Excuse* me?" The woman at the drugstore counter was young and blond . . . a few years older than us, and looked peeved.

"Um, yeah," I said. "Where's your non-script allergy medicine?"

"You mean nonprescription?" She raised her thin eyebrows. They were brown. Meaning her blond hair was fake. But then again, who am I—of the purple locks—to judge?

"Exactly." I smiled to make her feel simultaneously good and impolite.

"Exactamundo," Maria said. I tilted my head to the side. The lady looked at us as if we were mutants. We were teenagers. Close enough.

"Aisle seven," she said.

"Thanks a bunch!" I saluted and Maria waved. She gave us a half grin. Most people are genuine at their cores once you get past the façade.

"Benadryl, Benadryl, it's not my friend-a-drill," Maria sing-sang as I looked through the stacks of plastic bottles.

"Why's that?" I grabbed a bottle of Benadryl and walked back to the register manned by the bleached-blond cashier. It was a good dye job. I'll give her credit for that.

Maria said, "Once I took two tablets before a test because my eyes were really watery."

"So?" I handed the bottle to the cashier and she rang me up.

"Six-fifty-two."

I handed her a ten.

"*So?*" Maria was aghast. "Don't you ever read the side effects? It makes you sleepy. I could barely concentrate on my own first name let alone the themes in *The Scarlet Letter*!"

"Awful book." I shook my head and grabbed my change and medicine.

"You're telling me. Maybe it wasn't the Benadryl that

6

knocked me out, after all. You should pop one of those on the van ride over." She held the door open, and we continued on our journey home.

"I won't need one. With Zeke as a companion—"

"That's right! Zeke! I almost forgot."

"In all honesty, I'm kind of freaked about the whole thing." I tipped the pack of M&Ms into my mouth and finished them off. "I get a bit paranoid in the dark."

"No way!"

"For serious. Remember when Iggy asked me out to the movies?"

"The disastrous date. I do recall that. You refused to explain why."

I sighed deeply. "There was a blackout in the theater. We're sitting in total darkness and then all of a sudden we hear, 'Everyone, stay calm, stay calm!' Of course, I wasn't calm at all. It was weird to hear people talk without seeing their faces. Meanwhile Iggy was trying to turn it into a romantic moment. He started whispering stuff in my ear—not even romantic stuff, just ordinary mundane talk. Like 'My mom's cooking pasta for dinner tonight.' The whole thing was creepy and embarrassing."

I could tell Maria had actually been interested in the story, because she hadn't interrupted once.

"Wow."

"I know."

"Maybe all that talk of his mom's pasta scarred you for life. Can you still eat linguini?"

"Har-de-har-har." I rolled my eyes. "I'm not saying that experience is what made me afraid of the dark. I'm using it as an example to show you just *how* afraid of the dark I am."

"It does get pretty dark down there in the caverns," she said. "I understand your anxiousness, Hutchenson."

"Not a drop of natural light." I said this more to myself than to Maria.

"That'll teach you to get over your fears really quick." She grabbed my bottle of Benadryl out of the plastic bag and shook it like a castanet.

"I don't want to go into the caves." When I had fears, I did everything in my power to avoid what caused them. *Conquer* and *vanquish* were words best reserved for faded, historic battles.

"Who are you?" She snorted. "What have you done with the real Kaida? You know who I'm talking about. The girl who wears tie-dyed shirts with no shame. The young lass with the purple hair who actually makes polite conversation with homeless men? The Kaida who—"

"Thank you, thank you. Your flattery is much too kind. I'm not scared of our classmates and I'm not scared of homeless men."

"Yet you're scared of caves." She chucked my chin and made a turn onto my street. "Well, then Carlsbad could indeed be—to quote the estimable Principal Warwick—an educational experience for you."

"Maria. Maria!"

"I'm just saying. Stalagmites and whatnot. It could be all right. Hey!"

"What?"

"You could bring your flute. I could bring my violin. C'mon! How sweet would it be to say we jammed in a cave?"

"Can you really call what we do 'jamming'?" We stopped in front of my house, and I extracted my key, which was hidden under my headband.

"Can and will," Maria answered.

I unlocked my door. The lock clicked and pinged. I love the noise of home, more harmonious than anything I could play on the flute. "My irrational fear of the dark will be the most heart-stopping thing during the whole experience. It's going to be an atomic bore. And on top of that"—I opened the door—"I'm going to be spending a bucketful of time with Zeke and Tallon."

Maria slid her backpack off her shoulders and held her arms open. I fell into them, resting my head on her muscular shoulder. Maria was fond of lifting my brother's weights. So much so that she bought her own set of ten-pounders. "I'll come over tomorrow and make sure you're not packing anything so shredded and tattered that it'll disintegrate on your body."

"You're a good friend." I smiled, left her embrace, and shut my door.

It was only in my room that I could have safe darkness. It was there, in my own space, where I controlled everything. In my own universe, I could make darkness comfortable, something soft and enveloping, like a king-size flannel blanket. Something you looked forward to after a hard day.

But in a cave darkness was black and suffocating, a force that pressed and constricted your body, crunching your bones and deflating your lungs. And no matter how hard you screamed, it kept on . . . squeezing tighter . . . sharper . . . harder . . . on and on . . . until you felt as if you were nothing at all.

2

Wednesday through Sunday: five glorious days without school
even if it meant being stuck in a van with Zeke Anderson and
Joy Tallon. So far, they were okay.

"I like your hair," Zeke said.

I couldn't tell whether or not he was being facetious. I gave
him a close-lipped smile. "Thanks."

"Was it always that way?"

"You're kidding me, right?"

"I don't mean the color, I mean the style."

I looked out the window. There was nothing but an

expanse of brown, tan, and beige spangled with small bursts of dark green.

"You mean long?"

"Long and, like, you know . . ." his voice faded just like civilization had done a few hours ago. The terrain was endless and desolate, and occasionally a wind-whipped dust devil swirled across the roadside. It was enough to make a person hallucinate.

Poor Mr. Addison—one of my favorite teachers—was stuck driving solo because Mr. Lahte, his codriver, had come down with the flu. The trip from our town was around ten hours of straight driving, but we had made a few stops along the roads. Our last oasis had been a general store somewhere near the Arizona/California border. I had purchased some Coyote Cream because my skin felt as dry as parchment. And now we were driving past nowhere and nothingness. We were scheduled to stop for the night somewhere near the New Mexico border, but we still had a few hours to go.

Zeke's eyes were swimming-pool blue, custom designed to match his swim team status. He was tall and so long limbed that he verged on gangly. He was cute, not in the way mothers commented on, but in the way teenage girls commented on. He had a pretty girlfriend named Leslie Barker. She was thin but for two adorable rolls of fat on either side of her hips.

At the moment, Zeke's aqua eyes were vacant, roaming around my face.

"My hair wasn't always long," I answered. "When I was younger, it was short and shiny. Now it's a giant mess."

"It's not—"

I waved him off. "Yes, it is a giant mess. I like it like that . . . sort of."

His eyes wandered from my face into the rearview mirror, where we could both see Joy Tallon sleeping, sprawling over three seats. There were two rows in back, and she occupied the row right behind the driver. She was wearing white K-Swiss shoes with brown stripes.

Zeke leaned over and knocked her feet lightly, but she remained asleep. I unbuckled my seat belt and leaned over her seat. She was turned over on her side and there was a red splotch on her face where her fist had indented her cheek as she slept.

"I'm not blind over here, Kaida!" Mr. Addison called from the driver's seat. "Get down and put your seat belt on!"

"But you're going about seven miles per hour!"

"It's twenty-five, FYI, and even if we were going seven miles per hour, you'd still need to buckle up." The wind buffeted the car. Mr. Addison swerved to overcompensate. "Seat belt on now!"

I slumped back in my row and clanked my seat belt shut. As I heard its closing click, I also heard the metallic slide of another seat belt opening.

Joy sat upright, her head appearing in front of Zeke and me like we had conjured it up magically.

"Ms. Tallon!"

"What?" she croaked groggily. It sounded like "whote."

"Your seat belt!" Mr. Addison shouted back. He was a nice guy in his mid-forties. He had muttonchops that he should've shaved off a long time ago and wore a different hat each day to cover his bald head. In honor of the ride to the caves, he had on a Stetson cowboy hat. His age was revealed by the wrinkles around his eyes and mouth. I liked these kinds of wrinkles. They meant he had smiled and laughed a lot.

"Sit here, Joy," Zeke offered, patting the space between him and me.

"'Kay. You sure?" she grunted, but she was already up.

Zeke nodded.

"You sure, Kaida?"

"Of course."

She climbed over the barrier and plopped herself between us and fastened her seat belt. Her short, smooth hair grazed the bottom of her earlobes. Joy had an edgy haircut, with blunt, straight-across bangs and no other layers. She probably hadn't meant it to be cool, though. In her case, I figured that she hadn't changed it since childhood.

I looked out the window. Evening was morphing into night.

"You guys hungry?" Mr. Addison yelled toward us.

"Are we hungry?" Zeke questioned Joy and me.

"Nah," Joy responded.

"Not particularly." I had stuff in my bag and it was within reach. "I have some snacks and sandwiches, Mr. Addison. I can share. That way we don't have to stop and get food from the trunk."

"It's fine with me," the teacher answered. "Just keep yourselves buckled up. The winds out here are unpredictable."

I unzipped my bag and took out a tomato and cream cheese sandwich.

"Yum," Joy said.

"Here. Take it."

"What'll you eat?"

"I have a ton of stuff." I passed my bag to her. "Take whatever you want."

There was another identical sandwich, which I took. The rest of the food in my bag was mostly candy.

"What're you allergic to?" Joy shook my bottle of Benadryl.

"Pollen and dogs," I said. "It's also a bit of a sleeping aid."

"Got anything else nonsweet?" Zeke reached into my bag.

"Chips . . . pretzels. I'll share my sandwich with you."

"Me, too," Joy told him.

After thirty minutes we had eaten half my food and it had turned dark.

"My mom also packed me Benadryl," Zeke informed us.

"I think I'm going to take one. Sleep until we get there."

"Same."

Joy was already dozing off again, her round plump lips open. I looked out the window but couldn't make out anything more than lines and shadows. My eyes turned droopy. My skin felt fuzzy. I was falling asleep and I didn't try to fight it.

I was jolted awake by such sudden force, I thought something had exploded. My eyes sprang open.

Bam!

Bump, bump, bump.

Bam, bam!

It hit so hard and fast and so immediately that I didn't have time to think. Like a Chinese finger puzzle, the more I tried to pull out of it . . . to escape . . . the tighter everything became. Life seized up as if I were trying to run underwater. I was seeing things in slow motion . . . the collision, the tumbling of the van, the screams.

Suddenly it all stopped.

"Oh my God, oh my God!" Zeke was attempting to climb out of his seat, but he kept on running into bent metal. "I think we're upside-down. We've got to get out. . . . Move!"

He was screaming at me. "I'm trying!" I screamed back. My hands were desperately trying to untangle the snarl of seat belts, and I was still drowsy from the Benadryl. My body felt as if each muscle was slowly reassembling itself. "Joy?" I shouted. "Joy, where are you?"

Suddenly, I felt heat stinging me, the metal walls of the car hot to the touch. A flush of sweat drenched my body. My nostrils flared at the acrid smell of gasoline. My eyes homed in on a small orange flame. Somewhere in my drugged consciousness,

I knew I had ly seconds left . . . not minutes, just *seconds*. Still I moved like a turtle. I felt useless, like every time I tried to call a number on the phone I mixed up the order of the first three digits.

I spotted Joy crouching near the door, trying to open it to allow our escape. She yanked and yanked but nothing was happening.

I screamed to Zeke, "Help her!"

Zeke somehow managed to contort into an odd angle, stretching his long limbs until his spidery fingers wrapped around the hot door handle. He bit his lip and jerked the metal upward. The door slid open. I managed to grab my bag before we tumbled out.

Then we ran away from the van.

This was the type of running you can't emulate through motivational speaking, through pushing yourself. Because this is the type of running that just comes, and after you've done it, you think, *How?* And of course, you have no answer.

I was shaking. The past hours melted through my system like a burned film reel. Someone was holding me. Who? Maria? Maybe even my mom? But when I pulled away, I saw no one around me. I was clutching myself, standing alone with nothing but unimaginable darkness starting to shroud me.

I heard sobs and looked around for the source. I made out the silhouette of someone shaking. I came closer and saw it was Joy, crying like she didn't want to be heard.

"H-hey," I murmured, and placed a hand on her elbow.

She wasn't aware enough to acknowledge me. She just shook and shook and shook until Zeke appeared and pulled Joy into his wiry arms.

"Over." He coughed. "All over."

I admired Zeke, at least for a moment. He was no older than I was but was trying to act more adult. Then I thought of the one adult who should have been with us.

"Mr. Addison!" I yelled.

Zeke flinched and let go of Joy awkwardly. His voice was a deep bellow. "Mr. Addison?"

Sky and ground could barely be differentiated. The darkness around us was smoky and infinite. Still, once our eyes adjusted . . . I saw it first.

"Zeke! Joy!" I was pointing to a spot far into the distance. How this space was so long, how we had managed to run it so quickly . . . I couldn't even begin to wrap my mind around it.

The orange flicker that I had witnessed from inside the van suddenly started feeding itself on spilled gasoline. Like an animal eating itself alive, it consumed and burned. And then the explosion! The noise it made . . . not like the crackle from a fireplace, but the roar of a feral beast. It was as if we were in an action film . . . some ridiculous he-man, macho piece of garbage that my brother would rent.

"*Mr. Addison!*" I cried out loud.

"N-n-no," Joy stuttered.

"Mr. Addison! Mr. Addison!" I called out. "He has to be around somewhere!"

Joy's teeth chattered, not that it was all that cold.

"It's Zeke! It's all of us! Mr. Addison where are you?" Zeke bellowed.

"Mr. Addison!" I yelled out.

"Mister!"

"Sir!"

"Jerry Addison!"

"Mister," I shrieked, "Jerry." I gathered up more air in my lungs, "Addison!"

We waited for a call back. We kept screaming until our voices were hoarse . . . until the futility of the situation dawned on us, although no one would articulate it out loud.

Zeke was sweating and shivering at the same time. "We should walk around and look for him."

"How is it that we got out together and he got out somewhere else?" I asked.

"He didn't get out," Joy told us.

Her tone was monotonous, as lifeless as the night.

3

"He didn't get out?" Zeke was in a panic. "What do you mean he didn't get *out*!" He kicked the ground with desperate anger.

"You don't know that," I told Joy. "Don't say that!"

"The car was completely mangled—"

"We got out!"

"Exactly," Joy said. "We got out. So where is he?"

"He's around here somewhere!" My tears were falling fast and furious. *Think, Hutchenson, think!* "Let's back it up. Every-one just shut up a moment and let's try to think!"

No one spoke, which made things even creepier. The only

thing that was now making noise was the fire—loud popping noises that expelled glowing embers upward like an erupting volcano. To drown it out, I started talking. "What happened exactly? I mean I know we crashed, but . . . how?"

"I'm pretty sure we hit something." Joy's voice wasn't much louder than a whisper.

"What about Mr. Addison?" I continued. "Should we go back to the car and check? Maybe he got flung out and needs us and . . ."

"Did you see him?" Zeke questioned.

"No," I responded.

Joy gulped. "I might've. I mean I think he was still in the car . . . or maybe between the car and a rock or maybe . . . Everything was getting hot and smoky."

"Oh, God." I felt sick.

"I—I really can't be sure . . ."

I twisted my shoe into the dusty ground. The desert was vast and completely alien. It was dark but not black because of the fire and the overcast night, the cloud-covered full moon providing some visibility. I couldn't make out any bugs or beasts, but we all knew that terrible things were out there. I felt an electric breeze run over my face, blowing my hair in all directions. Up above, the winds were pushing the clouds across the sky.

"Okay." I drew a line in the dust of the desert. "Let's think."

They continued to breathe heavily and say nothing.

"Okay." I rubbed my hands together and then clapped them, trying to signify something official. "Where's everyone else from our school?"

"Driving miles ahead of us." Zeke groaned.

"Or miles behind us," I answered. "Our small van could have moved quicker than the big vans they were using. So maybe all we have to do is wait until they catch up."

"Does anyone have a phone?" Joy inquired.

"Mr. Addison made us pack them in the trunk of the van so we wouldn't be on the phone, blah, blah, blah." Zeke sat down and banged his head against the fold of his arms. He was right. All of our luggage and provisions had been incinerated. I had my messenger bag and Zeke had his backpack. Joy had escaped empty-handed. Everything else was gone.

"Check your bag, Kaida," Zeke prodded. "Just in case."

I groped around, but my phone wasn't there. "It's freaking black." Actually more like a subdued navy. I heard rustling and saw the faint outline of Zeke's hands searching through his own backpack. A click sounded and a bright beam shone.

"Wow—" I shielded my eyes.

"Aha!" he shouted comically. "It works!" The light focused on me, then my bag. "Now look for your phone!"

I opened my beautiful, worn bag and sifted through my remaining possessions lovingly. I discovered I had a flashlight, too—thanks, Mom!—and quickly extracted it. I turned it on. "Let's all go through our stuff. You know, to see how much food we have, etcetera."

"Good idea," Zeke agreed.

We sat down on the dusty ground and rifled through our bags. For the next two minutes, the silence of the desert was broken as we tore through items, hoped, waited, listened for some car motor or anything that signified salvation.

"No," I stated dryly. "No phone."

"What do you have, Hutchenson?"

"Where's Joy?" I panicked. I hadn't heard her voice for a few minutes.

"I'm here."

"Stop pacing and sit down," I told her. "We need to stick together."

She sat. Her face was wet and she was still shaking. It dawned on me that she was walking to burn off all that nervous energy. "I didn't bring my bag. That was stupid."

"Who had time?" I told her.

"Did you find anything, Kaida?" Zeke asked me again.

"Yeah." I focused my flashlight on the ground. Inside my bag was a thrift-shop sweatshirt that said *Dance! Dance!* in loopy black scrawl. I also had a poncho, the ugly yellow kind you beg your mom not to pack. Thank goodness Mom ignored my wishes. I had packed Benadryl, but it must have fallen out somewhere. Food-wise, I had pretzels, a bag of potato chips, and lots of candy, along with two bottles of water, which were now worth their weight in gold. I turned to Zeke. "How about you?"

Zeke gestured at his pack. There was another sweatshirt,

blue and crumpled. Another poncho, but his was red. He had some Cheez-Its and Doritos and another couple bottles of water. He also had a GPS, probably the most useful thing either of us had managed to bring. Suddenly I felt like I was suffocating and I began to cry.

"I feel like I'm in a bad movie." Joy rubbed her arms. Then a small light flicked by her face.

I ignored Joy's words and focused on the pinpoint of sparkling orange by her cheek. What was that? A firefly, maybe? The strong, shady scent of tobacco filled my nostrils, and I was absolutely baffled.

"Wait . . ." I stared at her. "You forgot your bag. You didn't sneak in your phone. But you have a lighter and a cigarette?"

"It's a disposable lighter. It costs less than a dollar. I had two smokes left in my pocket. I didn't even know I had them."

"A disposable lighter?" Zeke cried.

Joy blew out a cloud of smoke in response. I always wondered if people actually puffed out smoke rings in real life, or if actors just did that in movies.

"How many times can you use it?" he pressed.

She flicked it on and off several times. Nothing came out. "It's empty . . . disposable." In the dark, Joy's face was shadowed. All I could see of her were the wispy ribbons of smoke veiling her eyes. "Who cares?" Her voice had become less quivery.

"We could have used that! Suppose we get cold—"

"Zeke," I interrupted, "We're not cold now . . . it's over. Forget it, okay?" I rolled my eyes, annoyed with both of them.

"Our best bet is to wait by the side of the road. Back where the van is."

Zeke said, "I'm not going back there. What if the van explodes again?"

I wanted to punch him. I had socked Iggy once and he said I packed a powerful hit. Zeke was strong, but he was also skinny. A string bean I could boil.

"Got a better idea?" Joy countered.

"Fine." Zeke gave in. My flashlight found him and he raised his arms in the air. "Fine! You want to wait by the road? Fine. Whatever. I'm following you."

The van was still in flames and gave us enough illumination, so we turned off our flashlights to save the batteries.

"If we need fire," I said, "we got plenty of it there."

"That's toxic," Zeke decided.

"Fire's fire," I insisted.

"That's why you don't make the honor roll, Kaida," Zeke retorted.

I do make the honor roll, by the way. I was going to tell him, but what was the point? "I don't know if that fire is or isn't toxic, but it's warm and I'm getting cold and unless you have any other bright ideas, just shut up, okay?"

"Mr. Addison is burning in that fire," Joy muttered.

"I said, shut up!"

When no one spoke, the silence was worse than their stupid comments. Sometimes I wished my tongue would fall off. Joy started picking at her nails. Then she looked at the ground. Then she looked at the fire. Then she looked at the ground again. Her attention span was erratic, but none of us was focusing too well. "We should get going," I told the gang.

"Whatever," Zeke repeated. He clearly liked the word.

He picked up his backpack and I picked up my messenger bag, and off we went.

"It's probably like this," Joy spoke into the velvet night.

"What?" I asked as we walked toward the road.

"Being homeless," she replied.

"Jeez, Tallon, can you turn off the pessimism long enough for me to amass a grain of hope?" Zeke snapped.

Joy lifted her pointy shoulders in response. She looked like a muffin to me. Her jeans pulled at her belly, making her chub ooze out of her waistband. Her face was angular, her chin pinched. But her eyes were round, sort of doe-like, à la Audrey Hepburn. Her nose was sloped, with a bulb at the end of it.

"I think Joy's comments were insightful," I told him.

"Could you not be sarcastic for like five seconds?"

"I'm not being sarcastic. I don't have the energy to be sarcastic."

"Wrong. You're always sarcastic," Zeke said.

I don't think he was trying to be hurtful, but it still made me feel bad. I didn't want to be known as the world's most jaded teenager. But that's what my mom calls me some-times . . . because of the things I say. The problem is she doesn't hear the things I think.

"We feel like crap tonight, but homeless people always have

26

to feel this way," I continued. "Maybe we could discuss Joy's point together. We could expand on it like we do in English class, analyzing one measly quote. Maybe it would occupy us while we wait for some phantom car to toot along, pick us up, and save us from moldering in the Arizona desert . . . or maybe we're in New Mexico already."

No one said anything. I saw the road and pointed it out to the others.

"Right you are," Zeke crooned. His charm, along with his hope, was turned on again. We trudged to the edge of the roadway and we stood very close to the asphalt ribbon. If we did that in L.A., we'd get plowed over, but there was nothing out here. Not even a scampering rodent, a slithering snake, or a bug. I'd never felt so alone.

We had walked some distance from the fiery van, but the air was singed with the smell of burning rubber and gasoline. It was making me nauseated.

Please, something move! Anything! How about a tumbleweed? Deserts have lots of tumbleweeds!

Thoughts drifted through my brain.

You're going to die!

I felt more wind on my cheeks. It was stronger this time and it was kicking up dust and grit that stung my face. In the distance, things began to move. It was my tumbleweeds. They started to skitter over the desert surface.

The sky grumbled.

Uh oh!

The three of us looked at one another.

Abruptly the winds turned fierce. More grumbling skies, only it was getting louder and louder. I thought back to my earth sciences class.

Sudden storms often appear near the Rocky Mountains as air travels over the peaks, causing turbulence—

The skies cracked open! Lightning veins hit the ground not more than a hundred yards away. We all jumped and screamed.

"Oh, God." Joy held her face with her hand.

"You're kidding me, right?" I yelled to the sky. Rain started to drizzle down as if someone up there was salting us with water droplets.

Zeke growled out a slew of obscenities. He turned on his flashlight and so did I, hunting around for shelter—a tree, a rock, a cave—anything to prevent us from getting soaked. Then he said, "There's something over there." He homed in on the dark blob with his flashlight. It appeared to be a cluster of giant boulders.

We made a break for the area and we got lucky. It wasn't just rocks, it was an entrance to a cave. That shouldn't have surprised me—we were in cave country—but it did. We backed inside and watched as rain fell. First it was just big heavy drops, then the rain got thicker and denser until water cascaded down the mouth of our shelter.

We huddled together for warmth, and for a few minutes no

one spoke. But that wasn't because we weren't thinking about things.

After Iggy's sister had left for college, he had inherited her room along with her canopy bed. Rather than destroying the canopy as any sane teenage boy would've done, he kept the pink bed—along with the canopy—and painted the rest of his room black. He hung up metal posters. I loved his pink canopy. *That's where we are,* I told myself as we crouched together, *under Iggy's pretty canopy.*

We shivered in silence. Then I realized Joy and Zeke were gripping my fingers.

"Gah!" Joy yanked her hand from mine.

"What?" Zeke and I asked frantically.

"Something's leaking!" she cried. "I just got soaked!"

And then I felt a splotch of water on me. As I peered out of the cave, I was surprised to see what a downpour looked like. We had rain in California, but not this kind of rain. It really did fall in sheets. It looked like a big pane of glass ready to shatter on us.

"I thought this was a desert," Joy shouted over the noise.

"Torrential downpour," I quoted from Mr. Wren's science packet, "common to the area."

As if we were magnets, we banded together once again, our arms and heads finding the crevices of one another's bodies.

"Let's back up a little," Zeke suggested. "It's probably dry farther inside."

And this was where we made our first mistake. We walked backward. We could have—we should have—turned around and walked forward, but in times of peril people panic and disregard their usual habits. So we backed up, going deeper into the cave.

Our second mistake was not using our flashlights.

Our third mistake was taking too big steps.

Joy Tallon had not taken the Benadryl. She should have been more alert. But in the darkness, none of that mattered. All we heard was Joy's scream.

Joy had just made the fourth mistake.

4

Screams are like strings. Sometimes they're thick and fat, sturdy and strong. Sometimes they're thinner and braided like yarn. And sometimes they're like sewing thread, so skinny that they barely withstand any pressure before snapping. Joy had covered the full range of screams—from fat to skinny—all in a matter of seconds, just by saying the word *no*!

"Zee-yeek!" she screeched with a voice so shrill as to almost break. "Kay-duh-haw!"

My reaction was a millisecond quicker than Zeke's. I reached out and grabbed onto something. It felt like a person, but who knows? Whatever it was, it tugged me forward until I fell on my stomach. The heavy mass was dragging me toward a big, black hole. I wanted to let go, but I knew I couldn't do that without losing Joy.

I screamed. She screamed. A second later, my dreadful skid was abruptly stopped.

Someone was holding my legs, digging sharp nails into them.

"I got you!" Zeke yelled from behind. "I got you, I got you. Just stop struggling!"

My legs ached with an excruciating pain. My stomach had been sandpapered by the rocks and mud. My chin and forehead were scraped raw. But mostly my arms were numb from trying to keep Joy from falling.

"Relax," Zeke barked at me. "I'll try to pull you both up."

I'm 5'2" and weigh 124 pounds. Joy weighed a little more, but I didn't have any better ideas, so I said nothing. I now knew the true meaning of the phrase "eat my dust."

"Ready?" Zeke didn't wait for me to answer. Encircling his long fingers and rubbery palms around my ankles, he started to drag me away from the pit.

I tried to hold on to Joy. She tried to hold on to me.

Too heavy. Joy slipped out of my reach. She let go and screamed.

Her scream seemed to go on forever, but in fact it was just a second. Both Zeke and I heard the plop.

I screamed into the hole. "Joy, can you hear me?"

"Yes, I can hear you. I can't see anything."

Zeke quickly got out the flashlight and shone it into the pit. It appeared to be just deep enough so Joy couldn't climb out. "Are you all right?"

Joy looked into the spotlight, her face blackened with mud. She appeared to be holding herself. "I hurt my arm."

"Is it broken?"

"I dunno, but it hurts. Maybe I just pulled something." Her eyes frantically searched around. "Get me out of here!"

Zeke said to me, "I've got an idea. I'll grab your ankles and lower you into the pit. You grab on to her arms, and I'll pull you back up."

"Didn't we already try that?"

"Yeah, but we didn't plan it properly. You didn't have a good grip on Joy, and I didn't have a good grip on you. I almost lost my footing."

I was silent.

"If you've got a better plan, I'm listening."

I didn't have a comeback. We positioned the flashlight so we could see Joy and explained our rescue attempt to her. She was still gripping her arm, but what choice did we have other than to proceed?

"What if we all fall in?" I asked Zeke.

"Well, you can stay here with her and I'll try to get help—"

Joy screamed another no. "You've got to get me out of here!"

It was still raining waterfalls outside. The sky was crackling like a cherry bomb. I sighed. "How about if I lower my messenger bag down and see if she can grab it? Then we can both try to reel her in."

Zeke thought it was worth a try. As soon as we tried to pull her up, the strap broke. Joy fell backward and landed on her tailbone. By now, she was wailing.

Back to Plan A.

Zeke dangled me upside down and lowered me into the pit. I felt like something about to be fondued.

"Grab Kaida's hands!" Zeke called out to Joy.

"Trying!"

"Right . . . here." I was waving my hands around. The inside of the pit was inky black and ominous. Joy's outline looked like something from an ultrasound, like she was made of liquid metal.

I felt fingers gripping around my wrists. "We've got her!" I whooped. "Pull, Zeke, pull!"

Blood swam to my head. My brain started to go all fuzzy and my left hand began to tingle. Something in the way Zeke was holding my legs and Joy was holding my arms . . . too tightly.

"Got us?" I choked in a nasally voice.

He didn't answer. I heard the sound of rubber against earth.

"Zeke?" I persisted. My hand was losing sensation. I felt like I was dreaming, drugged. He started to pull us upward. "Go, go, go!"

"Hold on! Give me a second!" he yelled as an answer. Then he swore. I heard more scrapes against the ground.

"I've got this," he shouted to Joy and me. "I've got it—"

"Then get it!" Joy screamed.

"I'm trying, damn it!"

We were good for about three seconds. And then Zeke lost it, the three of us plummeted back into the pit, and the earth devoured us like some kind of biblical plague. A low growl rumbled in the background, the sound of something collapsing.

"Ow!" I said.

"Gah!" Zeke said. "What the—"

Joy wailed out, "Oh, God! We're going to die, we're going to die!"

"Stop it!" I told her. "We're not going to die."

But we *were* going to die. That much I knew.

"You're sitting on me, Kaida," Zeke said dryly.

"Sorry," I muttered.

"No problem."

"That's a good one." I laughed. "No problem. *Au contraire, mon ami.* The problem is monumental."

"I'm sorry." Zeke sounded on the brink of tears.

"It's not your fault, Zeke. It's not anyone's fault. It's just . . ." My voice trailed off. "Can anyone see, or am I stunned from the fall?" I asked, feeling around.

"No, it's pitch-black," Zeke replied. "I took off my backpack to pull you guys up. Now we don't even have a flashlight!"

"My messenger bag!" I shouted. "*My* flashlight's in *my* bag and my bag is down here somewhere!"

We all started groping around. We literally couldn't see our hands in front of our faces. It was the most enveloping, evil darkness I had ever experienced, and I had to constantly talk out loud to myself to keep from panicking.

"You're okay, you're okay, you're okay, you're okay . . ."

"Found it!" Zeke shrieked. With a flick of a switch we had illumination. I looked at Zeke's face and saw the curve of his mouth set downward, his turquoise eyes half closed in misery.

"What now?" he asked.

"Shine the flashlight above us," I suggested. "Maybe we can climb back up."

He did. Several rocks had fallen on top of our entrance, blocking our escape path. I felt the surrounding walls. They were wet and steep.

No way out.

"Don't panic," I said out loud. "Panic doesn't do any good."

No one spoke. Finally Zeke asked, "What now?" I took the flashlight from him and moved it around. Joy was rocking in a fetal position. She was beyond panic.

"I really screwed up," Zeke choked out.

"It's not your fault, Zeke," I told him. "This was just a bad situation that kept turning worse. If the van hadn't crashed, we wouldn't have been in the rain. The rain led to the cave, the cave to Joy's fall. Joy's fall to . . ." I trailed off. "What's the use? Let's think up another plan. At least it'll keep our brains occupied!"

"You okay?" Zeke was crouching by Joy. She looked like a cornered animal.

"My arm," was all she said in response. "I hurt it in the fall and then it got yanked."

I squatted down beside her and stroked her hair. It felt like silk. That's the most basic way to comfort a girl, by touching her gently. I had experienced this sort of aid a million times before.

"Joy," I asked softly, "are you bleeding?"

"I don't know."

"Can I pick up your arm?"

"No."

"Okay. It's okay," I tried to soothe her.

"It really hurts."

"I know," I crooned, "I can't even imagine." But I could. I broke my arm in sixth grade playing basketball. That had been the end of my athletic career.

Zeke started shining the flashlight over the walls. "Look. There are tunnels down here. Maybe we should wander around."

"Maybe we shouldn't do anything right now," I told him. "We're all too frazzled and too tired to think properly." I felt several pings on my head and looked up. The hole that we had slipped through was starting to cave in. "On second thought, maybe walking around is a better option than getting buried alive."

Joy let go with a wail. I said, "Can you walk, Joy? Is it just your arm or your legs, too?" I tucked a lock of hair behind her ear.

"I can't walk! I can't move!"

"I'll carry you." Zeke stretched out his arms.

"No, no," I insisted. Another bit of dirt crashed onto my skull. We had to get away from the spot and we had to do it now. The hole was beginning to leak pebbles and rocks. "Try to get up, Joy. I'll help you—"

"Don't touch my right arm!"

Zeke grabbed her waist and hoisted her to her feet. Slowly, he let go. "You can stand."

She nodded and took a step forward. "I'm okay. I can walk."

"Are you sure?" Zeke dusted off his pants.

"Yeah."

"Then let's get out of here . . . as in right now."

Zeke shined his flashlight around, and we walked into the tunnel. I could stand up inside, but Joy and Zeke had to bend over. A sharp odor plunged into my nostrils. The place felt diseased: chilly and clammy and without hope.

"In a place with light deprivation are creatures deformed?" I asked, half joking.

"What?" Joy asked, confused.

Zeke ignored her. "There's light here somewhere."

"Yeah, your flashlight," I retorted.

"It's not pitch-black," he insisted. "It can't be."

"There are undiscovered parts of the earth," I began, my voice not seeming to belong to me. "Not everything is safe."

I shivered at my own words.

"You're joking, but you're not joking," Zeke whispered.

"Why are you whispering?" But I was speaking quietly, too.

"I don't know," he answered. "I don't know. I don't know."

We continued to trek through the tunnel. Mercifully, it widened and heightened until Zeke and Joy could walk upright. I thought about these kinds of scenes on TV. At the end, something was always waiting. It could be a hermit who'd kill us just because we were there. Or undiscovered animals . . . creatures of the underworld. Maybe we'd be attacked by our own mental insanity. But surely something was waiting for us.

The pungent stench intensified all around us.

"God, what is that?" Joy gasped.

"Bat shit," Zeke answered. "I think."

"It's called guano," I added.

We walked on, the smell strangling us.

"Wait." Zeke suddenly gripped my hand.

"What?" I squeezed his hand back. Even though we weren't

the best of friends, his touch felt wonderful.

"Guano," he replied. "Guano! Lovely, lovely guano! Bat shit."

Joy regarded Zeke's slaphappy grin. "Maybe you should sit down?"

"You guys!" He was clearly frustrated. "Guano comes from bats!" He shook his head and turned directly to me. "Kaida, what have we been learning about the caves in science class?"

"You mean the Carlsbad Caverns?"

"Yes, exactly! What particular creature lurks inside these dark, dank caverns?"

"Bats," I said.

"And how do bats eat?"

"They fly out at dusk to feed and return in the morning to sleep," I answered. "Zeke, I don't see—"

"There's guano in this cave. That means there're bats in this cave."

I thought of bats and heard Maria's voice. *Rabies.* I kept my thoughts to myself. "We're all on the same page with that one, Zeke. Bats do live in caves."

"And presumably, like all bats, our bats get hungry?"

"One would assume."

"So . . ." He moved his hands, waiting for me to say something.

Guano . . . bats . . . bats have to feed.

It was the middle of the night. Meaning if our cave had bats, the bats were out feeding. Then it came to me like a lightbulb turning on. "There has to be an opening for the bats to fly in and out!" I shrieked.

He picked me up and swung me around. Then he clapped his hands together. "All we need to do is search. There *is* an opening somewhere!"

"What if the opening to the cave was what we fell through?" I asked him.

"Not big enough for bats to go in and out of. There has got to be a ton of bats, judging from the amount of guano. There should be another entrance. All we have to do is find it."

"Happy." Joy yawned. "Very happy."

"How can you be tired?" Zeke squealed.

I blushed in solidarity. "I don't know, Zeke. Maybe she's tired because it's God-only-knows how late." Something illuminated from Zeke's wrist—his wristwatch. "What time is it?"

"Two in the morning."

"We're more likely to find the opening when the bats fly into it at dawn. Why don't we just rest and conserve our energy for a while?"

"But we're so close!"

"It'll be easier to follow the bats . . . and the sun will come out and . . ." My eyelids fell steadily. I felt dreamy and groggy.

"I agree." Joy sat down, leaned against the walls, and closed her eyes.

Zeke yawned. Our exhaustion was contagious. "Okay.

We'll take a nap." He sat down between us. "Just a *nap*," he enunciated. "I'm going to set my watch. We've got to get up in a few hours, all right?"

I agreed. Nothing better to do.

He turned off the flashlight, and with that out went consciousness.

I heard: Hi, hi, hi, in a wispy voice.

Then someone shook me awake. Zeke's voice. "We've got to get going. It's five in the morning. We've got to find the bats."

"Why don't we just let the bats find us?" I croaked, rubbing my eyes.

Zeke turned on the flashlight and shined it in my eyes. Then he woke up Joy. It took several minutes to leap back to consciousness, and when I did, a heavy despair smothered me like a wet towel. We were in the same nightmare as before the nap. If I had been alone, I probably would have sunk back down into sleep and died. But other people were depending on me and I was depending on other people. No one could let the next person down.

"Let's go searching!" Zeke clapped several times. He had that kind of instant adrenalized energy—quick to come and quick to wear off. Joy's enormous eyes moistened and I gazed at her. She caught my stare and shook it off.

We managed to stand and began to walk forward.

"Bucky's gonna get sued for this." Zeke was calling our illustrious school by its popular endearment.

"Buchanan *was* the president who never did anything," I quipped.

"You know who's probably worrying about me right now?" Zeke asked as I looked at our surroundings. More and more endless cave, dark and unpromising.

"Your parents?" Joy offered.

"Leslie," he answered.

An image of Leslie splashed into my mind. But she wasn't smiling openmouthed as she usually did. Instead she was glaring, her face and body wretched. This is what happens when you're afraid. You see and remember things as being distorted . . . terribly frightening. Pictures flutter through your mind and your breath catches. If people are around you, they look at you strangely.

Joy touched my back and I jumped.

"Whoa," she said.

"Sorry," I mumbled, "just freaking myself out."

"You looked like you were having a seizure, only the kind where you don't roll around and stuff."

I nodded.

"I'm doing that, too, Kaida," Joy offered sympathetically. "Freaking myself out."

"You guys are weird." Zeke snorted.

I felt my face go hot. "You never do that? You never think

43

about something scary and get freaked out? You're not scared right now? I don't think so!"

"Calm down—"

"You're not freaked?"

"Of course I'm freaked!" he shouted. "But there's nothing I can do about it, so shut up, okay? You sound possessed or something." He quickened his pace and I wondered if maybe I *was* possessed.

"I grant you permission to perform an exorcism," I said. My voice was like porcelain, white and breakable. I felt like a ghost.

"God, leave me alone!" he groaned.

But he sounded terrified.

"You were the one who came up with the idea," Joy reminded him.

"Thank you so much for bringing that up."

"Just saying."

"Of course you were."

They bickered for another five minutes while I felt my chewed nails. I'm a nail biter, I admit it. And who could ask for a better time to bite them—except my hands were gross and dirty. My thumb was okay. As I raised it to my mouth, bright flecks appeared on my hand. I rotated my wrist, fascinated by what I was seeing. Then I pulled my hand to my side and the bits of illumination fell to the ground as if I'd dropped them. Joy and Zeke were still going at it.

"Guys!" I interrupted.

"What?" they yelled in unison.

"Look at the ground!" They instantly stopped fighting. No one spoke.

"That's light," I told them.

"It's on my leg," Joy whispered. Her leg was starting to streak with a vibrant pink. The kind of coral associated with dawn.

"My shoes." Zeke lifted his feet, the light then spreading to the ground.

"My arm."

"The ground in front of me."

The flashlight was no longer our only source of light.

"Forward?" I suggested.

"I second it," Joy agreed.

"Third it," Zeke answered.

We waited a brief moment before charging ahead. Not walking but running. Racing. The light grew as we progressed farther, becoming wider and brighter until it was blinding. But we didn't stop. We kept running. A deafening buzzing started to sound, like radio static; no, more like the obnoxious kind of feedback that comes when a microphone is held too close to a speaker. I couldn't hear the sound of my own feet. I couldn't feel my feet moving. Because they weren't moving.

There was a blinding flash of light as if my entire world was exploding. Suddenly we were flying. My whole body was flying . . . falling . . . plunging down into an endless abyss. It was the kind of sudden vertical fall that sent your head spinning and your stomach jolting and shot a shivering pain into your body from your temples to your toes.

5

This morning's wake-up song was something by Metallica.

Ha ha, I thought, *my brother's idea of a practical joke—except it was coming from the radio.* I croaked and banged my alarm clock, of course missing the stop button and just hurting my hand.

Exit: light
Enter: night
Take my hand
We're off to never, never land!

I smashed my fist on my clock again. It still didn't stop screeching.

I finally got out of bed and pressed the stop button. I felt sore, my arms and legs stinging with pins and needles. I tend to put my arms behind my head when I sleep. It's an awful habit. I was also unusually sweaty.

I went into the bathroom and looked into the mirror, thinking about the multiple man-looking-in-mirror literary clichés.

"She looked into the mirror," I said aloud. "Staring back at her was a groggy adolescent with dried drool on her face."

I turned on the hot-water tap and waited for it to heat up. In the meantime, I brushed my teeth, noticing that I was out of toothpaste and mouthwash.

Yuck.

When I looked in the medicine cabinet for a spare, it was just about empty, holding a bar of soap and my rosewater perfume.

Where are my Advil and Benadryl—and my toothpaste?

I was confused and I knew why. I had a very vivid nightmare last night. It was still impacted in my brain as I washed my face. My skin appeared to be flaking around my eyes and nostrils. I looked at the bathroom countertop and found a tube of moisturizer marked Coyote Cream, with a howling coyote silhouette.

How'd I get this?

I shrugged as I studied the tube. I always enjoy reading the backs of cosmetic products. They're usually pretty funny.

48

Like on the back of shampoo, you'd think they were describing some elite eco-environment.

It read:

Coyote Cream is a soothing moisturizer with aloe vera and desert botanicals. Apply daily or as often as desired. The calming mixture helps quell rashes and dryness. The secret is the essence of the New Mexican desert, the Land of Enchantment's mystical and herbal cures.

Wouldn't something from a desert make my skin drier?

As I tentatively applied the cream to my face, I was reminded of the Carlsbad Caverns and my class trip. Maybe that was where my Advil and Benadryl had gone. Maybe Mom had already packed my medicine even though the trip was a little over a week away. That would be typical of my over-preparing mother.

I wondered if they had assigned the van groups yet. I was praying that by some stroke of luck, I'd be with Maria.

"Anyone but a jock," I said, slathering the creamy lotion on my face.

The jocks in my grade were mostly all right, just boring. Roger Patterson . . . Zeke Anderson.

I squeezed more moisturizer onto my face, applying liberally. Zeke. Why did I keep thinking about him?

Abruptly, my mind flooded with a heavy darkness. A crash. A storm. A cave. I dropped the Coyote Cream and stood upright, paralyzed.

No. Absolutely not. Impossible.

"Dude, what are you doing in there? Last night's dinner was plain old macaroni," my brother shouted while pounding on the bathroom door.

I opened the door and he began to crack up.

"What's on your face?" He laughed. "Looks like butter or something. Did you have trouble eating your breakfast? Not that big of a deal, Kaida. Just put the fork in your mouth."

"What are you talking about?" I touched my cheek and remembered the Coyote Cream. Like me, Jace was still in his pajamas. Flannel pants and an Iron Maiden T-shirt.

"Look . . . uh, where was I last night?"

He squinted, his eyes the same gray color as the bathroom tile at school. "Kaida," he began sternly, "who got you drunk? Seriously. If it was freaking Maria, I'm gonna kill her!"

"I wasn't drunk. I don't drink. The only thing I drank last night was water, Jace—"

"Vodka!" he roared. "Bet you drank vodka!"

There are a million translucent beverages. But to my brother there was only one.

"What are you talking about, Jace? I drank water. Wah-tur."

Jace was still skeptical.

"So I was home last night? I didn't just get back from, um, the hospital, or anything?"

He gave me a strange look. "What?"

"Never mind."

"You didn't just get back from . . ." He waved his hands, motioning for me to finish his sentence.

"Like the hospital or something."

He continued to stare at me. Then he knocked my head with his fist. "Get out of the bathroom. I gotta brush my teeth."

I obeyed. "But really I was home—"

"We have vodka at home, too." He bent down and picked something up. "Is this yours?"

It was the Coyote Cream. "Yeah, I guess."

He rolled his eyes. "Are you an idiot?"

"I'm getting a no for that one."

"Then why are you using this crap?"

"It's not crap—it's all natural."

He read the ingredients. "Never heard of this brand. Where'd you get it?"

"I found it in the bathroom."

"Well, just in case . . ." He squeezed out all the contents in the toilet, then wrapped up the tube in tissue and dropped it in the trash. "Stick to the old brands, okay? Don't want any trouble, right?"

I was too stunned to respond.

Jace said, "I've gotta brush and dry my teeth. "

Dry my teeth? I thought. But before I could ask him about it, he shut the door in my face. Just like that, without another word.

"Mom?" I said, looking up from my breakfast. Waffles with chocolate syrup—my mother was in a jovial mood.

"Mmm?" she answered. My mother wore acid-washed jeans and a black T-shirt. I kind of preferred she'd just stick to a dress or something.

"When's my class trip?" I stabbed my waffle and something oozed out of it.

"In about ten days."

"Did you pack my—"

"Soo-zee, don't cry," Mom cooed to my younger sister, who was sitting in her high chair. My sister had the fine blond hair and flawless skin that only graces the very young.

"I had the weirdest dream," I said loudly, trying to grab my mother's attention over the screaming infant.

"Do," she said between hushes, "tell." She scooped up my sister and started bouncing up and down, dancing around the kitchen and singing all sorts of maternal jingles.

"Well, it started off like—"

"Morning," my mom sang out. "It's mor-nin' and we're not so hah-ah-ah-ppy! Go on, Kaida," she urged, her voice still musical.

"You know, it's not that important, Mom. The waffles are good."

"Thank you." Mom huffed. Suzanne continued to wail, her face wrinkled like a golden raisin. "Stop crying, little miss."

"Mom, do you want me to take her for a minute?" Suzanne's habit was to wake up at three in the morning. Everyone except for Mom wore earplugs to sleep.

"No, no, I'm fine."

But Mom looked exhausted. I got up and carefully took Suzanne from her arms. The doorbell rang.

"I'll get it." I opened the door, knowing exactly who'd be there.

"Well, good morning to you too, Sue!" Maria twittered in response to my sister's shrieking. She was wearing a cotton minidress with suns dotted across it.

"Nice dress," Jace remarked as he descended the stairs and entered the kitchen. "Looks like acne."

"To match your face," Maria responded cheerfully.

Just get married already, I thought with annoyance. They were always doing this. Good for Maria, though; she was unflappable. She let herself in and grabbed Suzanne, lifting her body into the air. "Woooo!" she said, turning to me. "You about ready to get going?"

"About ready? I'm fully ready." I grabbed my messenger bag and noticed that, remarkably enough, Suzanne was quiet. Maria went into the kitchen and gave Suzanne to my brother, and as we left the house, her screams started once again.

"Kaida, I gotta hand it to you." Maria sighed as she looked at the sky. "You're a good sister." She bent down to tie her shoe. It was the quilted puffy kind and neon green.

"My mom's so exhausted. I worry about her sometimes."

"Worry?"

"You know, about her getting sick or—"

"*Stop* it, Kaida! Why do you want to ruin the day first thing in the morning?"

I had no comeback. It seemed that I was putting everyone in a bad mood.

Such is life when one is blessed with a winning personality.

6

We were almost at school. Maria had turned perky again. "Want to pick up Iggy? He's just a few houses away."

"Not in particular, no."

"Well, too bad, 'cause I already told him we would," Maria said. "You're in a mood. What d'you have against ol' Igg?"

"Nothing." I had wanted to be alone with Maria to tell her about my dream, but that wasn't going to happen.

When we arrived at a blue stucco house, Maria yelled, "Yo, Igg!"

Iggy peered out from his open bedroom window. He

looked like he had just gotten up. His red hair was a ridiculous afro.

"If you're in your pajamas, we're not waiting for you to change," I shouted.

"Change? I've been up for an hour," he said at normal decibel level. Even though his bedroom was on the second story, the distance up wasn't really that high. We could hear each other easily. "Wait up."

He descended in a matter of seconds.

"Did you dye your hair?" Iggy asked me as he closed his front door.

"Two weeks ago," I answered.

"Really?"

"Really. Thanks for noticing."

But that was Iggy . . . boys in general, I think. Iggy played the violin with Maria and me in orchestra. He was extremely talented, but it seemed to be the only thing he was focused on. He tended to space out for major periods of time. Like, say, months. . . .

"It's looking kind of purple," he told me.

"That's what I was going for," I retorted.

"Iggy, you're looking pale today," Maria said pointedly.

"Thanks, guys. You're great friends."

Bucky High lurched into view, its brick walls looking as prisonlike as ever. Zeke Anderson was leaning against an entry door, with Leslie Barker at his side, laughing and touching his arm. As Maria, Iggy, and I approached the building, Zeke glanced at us briefly, his eyes narrowing as they fell on me.

We locked eyes for a fleeting moment. Then he nodded in a typical jock salute and picked up Leslie, throwing her over his shoulder as she giggled.

"Hey, guys," I greeted them as I walked up the stoop.

"Hey," Leslie snorted, "how was your weekend?" Zeke put her down and she brushed something invisible off her jeans.

"It's Monday?" I wondered out loud.

Leslie raised her eyebrows. "You're serious?"

We stood there awkwardly. We might as well have been twiddling our thumbs and talking about baseball. Why were we talking? I turned around and met the confused stares of Iggy and Maria, still on the bottom of the steps. I had rushed ahead of them to greet Zeke and then wondered why.

"Bye?" I said like it was a question, and raced into school, my face hot. I felt a clamp on my shoulder and flinched.

"Kaida?" It was Maria's tanned hand that gripped my shoulder in a way that said either *We're concerned* or *What the hell?* Iggy stood a few paces behind her. The "foyer," as the administrators called it, was constantly packed with students, be it class time or not.

"Not like I have a problem with friendliness or anything, but . . ." Maria removed her hand from my shoulder and slung her arm around my neck. "Did you like . . . like ditch us over the weekend for the Zekester and his other half?"

"I was just saying hi, Maria—you should try it sometime," I joked. We had a word for this, the feeling of knowing that something should make sense and yet not being able to find that sense.

Confuzzled.

We started strolling to our lockers. They were red, which meant you were in tenth grade and not allowed to complain because you were not yet in the dreaded eleventh grade.

"Iggy thinks you're leaving him for Zeke." Maria sighed.

"I can't leave Iggy because I'm not currently with him—a minor glitch in that theory, huh?"

"So you do like Zeke! Is that why you went all . . . how does my dad say it?" She cleared her throat and spoke in a baritone voice. "Moony over him."

I laughed and shoved Maria into the freshmen lockers. They were yellow.

"Denial, denial," Maria tsked.

"Honestly, it's not that." A brown-haired freshie looked up at me cautiously. She blushed and turned away. Poor kid. Was I ever that scared of high school?

"What is it then, my dear?" Maria teased.

"He was in my dream last night."

"O-kay. So now you just dug yourself into a deeper hole. Like, a pit so perilous no amount of rope could get you out of it. A hole so—"

"Can you let me finish—"

"Do I really need to?" She snapped the strap of my camisole beneath my shirt and made a run for it. Strap-snapping is my ultimate pet peeve, and Maria knew this all too well. I wanted to hit her, but she was too quick on her feet.

I took off after her. When I'm running, I'm about as perceptive as a potted plant, and I collided with someone. Shock waves fired up my body.

I looked up and saw that the person was tall, about a head and a half taller than I was. He had silken wavy black hair and eyes the size of tea saucers—a very winning combination.

"Um, sorry."

I scanned his face. Nope. No recognition, and I was surprised. I had a built-in radar for good-looking guys. I walked past him. I felt like my nose was broken, and it already had a bump on it. Nothing tragic but plainly evident.

"You're just going to walk past me?" the guy called after me. "You seemed like you were in such a rush when you smacked into me!"

Cheeky, he was. How very endearing. I didn't turn around.

When I got to my locker, Maria was wiping beads of sweat off her face. They were iridescent, like tiny prisms. "Slow," she huffed. "You're slow today."

"You're no athlete yourself, dearest." I opened my locker and shoved books in and out of the space: *Englchemiforeignlangualgebra*. All my subjects blended after a while.

Down the hall I saw Mrs. Mimms lighting a cigarette, a wavy band of smoke trailing from her face. I nudged Maria. "Mrs. M is um, *smoking*."

She turned to look at Mrs. M, then squinted her Eurasian

eyes at me. "I don't get it, but some people can't get enough of it."

I said, "That's nicotine for you."

She looked at me like I had six heads. "Nicole who?"

"Maria, can you *stop*?" I snapped my head back. "You're not allowed to smoke indoors and she's a teacher—"

"Um, Kaida. Since when are you not allowed to smoke indoors?"

I crossed my arms and saw Mrs. M blithely light up Joy Tallon's cigarette, as casually as if she were picking up a dropped book.

"Am I in the twilight zone? Not only is that weird, it's totally illegal."

"Okay, Kaida, let us review," Maria told me. "A) it's not illegal, and B) since when did you care what's illegal and what's not illegal?"

I scratched my scalp. It was dry. It could use a good deep conditioning. "What have I ever done that's illegal? And don't say like, vandalize the school. Because everyone draws on their lockers."

She pulled up close to me and whispered, "Coyote Cream. Jace told me in the kitchen this morning I'd better keep my eye on you."

"What?" *Why had she been talking to my brother about me?* "Okay, that's definitely not—"

"Shut up!" she said. "Let's just talk about this later."

The last bell trilled and I couldn't find Maria.

"Hey," a tentative voice sounded behind me.

I turned around and faced the gangly, Gumbyesque figure of Zeke Anderson. "Sorry for acting weird this morning," I said, noticing that Leslie Barker and her mousy friends were staring at me.

"Yeah, no . . . it's fine," Zeke answered.

Yeah, no. What an odd sequence of words. And yet, right now, they were a succinct summary of how my day had been.

"I mean you weren't really acting weird." He started to touch my shoulder and then decided no, and pulled his hand back. "Look, can I walk you home?"

Leslie's eyebrows shot up. I'd never noticed them before, but they were arched.

"Sure, walk me home. But I live on Agatha Street. Don't you live—"

"Far away, but I think I need to talk to you."

"Your girlfriend looks like she's going to kill me. Or kill me and then you."

"I've explained it to her. Got all your stuff? Need to stop by your locker?"

"No, I'm all right."

He turned and waved to Leslie and a jealous smile formed with her pale lips. *Not to worry, Les, he's all yours.* "Let's just go straight home. Straight to my home, I mean."

We shot out of school until we were alone. "Okay . . . so don't get me wrong." He squinted as he looked up at the glaring sun. "You were kind of in my dream last night."

"Context, please." My heartbeat was a galloping horse.

"It was weird. Really, um—"

"Vivid," I interrupted.

Zeke gave me a sideways glance. We were on a street lined with stores. He stopped walking and leaned against the wall of a bagel store. "Yeah. Vivid. Really vivid. How did you know that?"

"I think I had the same dream."

A few cars whooshed by. I stared at the sidewalk, then began to cross the street.

"Kaida, watch out!"

Zeke ran and pulled me out of the street, but another person wasn't so lucky. I heard a screech and a scream and then a loud *thump*! In the middle of the road lay an injured man, vibrant red liquid splashed over his face and arms as if he'd been doused in ketchup. My hands went numb and my fingers felt like sandbags as I took out my cell phone and tried to dial the digits. But I couldn't get my mind to cooperate.

In the meantime, Zeke had whipped out his cell phone. "Omigod!" He dialed three digits. Presumably 911. Suddenly he took my phone away from my ear and dialed. "What the hell!" he stammered as he redialed. "It's—it's not connecting."

"Try again."

He did. "Nothing."

"Try my phone again."

Once again, Zeke redialed. "It's like . . . nothing!"

As I looked around, I saw cars coming and going. Although the passing traffic avoided the body, the vehicles continued on their way, oblivious of a bleeding body in the middle of the street.

Slow down, you idiots, my brain yelled out. *Yield!* There were a few people on the street. "Someone!" I sputtered ineloquently. "There's a man! A hit-and-run!"

Zeke flailed his arms. Everyone says when someone is hurt, you should scream. Nobody says that it's nearly impossible to do this. When something bad happens, it's hard to find your voice. It gets lost between your stomach and your feet. Somewhere in your thighs maybe.

Eventually we did scream, but no one came to help. We were screaming and jumping up and down, but everyone was ignoring us.

About five minutes later, a van pulled up—or something that looked like an ambulance, but snow white without a siren or any other typical ambulance markings. Instantly, the insane traffic had grounded to a halt, cars keeping a big distance from the accident scene. Pedestrians had suddenly disappeared.

Just me and Zeke and a dying man.

Four men dressed in bleached white garb got out of the vans. They had white hats on their heads and white aprons across their bodies and wore surgical masks on their faces. They looked like they had arrived from the morgue and were ready to do an autopsy except the man wasn't dead yet. I could tell because I heard moaning and his legs were still twitching.

They picked up the body with their latex gloved hands and put it inside the back of the van. There wasn't a gurney, and no one made any attempt to stop the bleeding. It looked to my untrained eyes as if there had been no medical intervention whatsoever. As the last of the men closed the hatch of the vehicle, he glared at the two of us.

"What are you lookin' at?"

"Me?" Zeke said. "Nothing, sir."

I was rendered absolutely speechless.

"Keep walking," he barked at us.

Immediately the two of us took off at a fairly decent trot. When we were safely away from the scene, I stuttered out, "W-what was that? *Who* was that?"

"I have no idea!" Zeke answered. "Maybe we should talk another time."

Without waiting for my answer, he took off like hunted prey. I stood stock still, my mind back on what had just happened. Throwing that poor man into the ambulance like he was a sack of garbage—like he wasn't human at all. My head pounded as hard as my heart was beating. What was going *on*? Did I fall and hurt my head? Was that the reason behind my weird dream? But what about Zeke's dream?

Was I dreaming now?

More like having a nightmare. I closed my eyes and saw only red. Those horrible men had started off dressed in white, but within seconds they had become soaked in scarlet.

They weren't afraid of blood, it seemed.

Or of death, for that matter.

7

Once, in a dream, I couldn't dial my own telephone number.
I punched numerical buttons in a myriad of orders, 3-6-8-2,
9-8-7-1, but nothing came out right. That's how I felt now. No
matter how I processed what had just happened, the events
remained twisted. The images . . . I couldn't shake them
loose.

When I got home, Jace was sitting on the family-room
couch, flipping through television channels. There was an
advanced physics textbook on his lap and several pieces of
paper sprawled out before him. My brother was wearing
khaki cargo pants and a white-turned-gray-from-too-many-

washings T-shirt. His hair was messy, probably from raking it with his fingers. He did that when he concentrated on schoolwork.

I stopped at the doorway between the kitchen and the family room, attempting to catch my breath. I was profoundly affected and if I approached Jace in the wrong way, he'd just accuse me of being hormonal or hysterical.

"Jace . . . I need to talk to you."

His eyes were still glued to the television. "Sure."

I sat on the couch. It was ugly but comfortable, igniting an ongoing debate between Mom and Dad as to whether it should be chucked or saved.

"This couch is a catalyst for so many arguments in this family." I was picking at my nails.

He looked up from the TV screen and regarded my face. "Somehow I don't think that's what you want to talk about."

Just get it all out. "I saw a guy get rammed by a car after school," I announced flatly.

"Ugh! That's messed up!"

"It was terrifying. And the worst part was that no one seemed bothered by it. Everyone around pretended it was no big deal." Except Zeke, and there was no reason to get him involved right now.

"The first time I saw something like that, I was freaked out, too." He turned down the television. "I understand." He seemed to be collecting his thoughts. "Speaking from older brother experience, I can tell you don't worry. It'll pass."

67

"Don't *worry*? There was blood everywhere."

Jace looked up me. "Didn't the cleanup crew show?"

"The cleanup . . ." My mind was whirling. "Some guys in white took him away in a van . . . is that what you mean?"

Jace looked at me as if I had just come from the moon. "It's over, Kaida. Don't talk about it anymore. It's messy stuff."

I was momentarily stunned. "Nine-one-one didn't work."

Jace looked at me with a puzzled expression. "Nine wha-what?"

"Nine-one-one." When Jace still didn't get it, I said, "You know, the emergency line." I paused. "What's *wrong* with you?"

Something inside him snapped. "Kaida, are you being provocative just to get attention? It's sad, but things like this happen all the time. It's part of life. Just deal."

"Thanks for being so understanding."

His eyes softened. "Look, I'm sure you were scared when you saw all that . . . mess. It must have been gross. But it's over. Stop worrying about it."

"Are you *crazy*?" I stared at him. "Am I crazy?"

"That's a very good question!" He became angry, grabbing his schoolwork and jumping off the couch like someone had lit his cargo pants on fire. "Maria did get you drunk." He heaved a disappointed sigh. "Kaida, this is part of your nasty little hangover. Go hydrate yourself!" He stomped to the stairs, but not before giving me a hard glare. "Stop talking, Kaida. Keep

68

your thoughts to yourself and your mouth shut tight."

That, I thought, *is something I have never been able to do.*

The next morning I met Maria right before first period. I wanted to tell her all about the accident, but she had a glazed look in her eyes.

"Feel." Maria pressed my hand to her throat. "It feels puffy."

"You have a cold, babe, take a sick day."

"Shhhh . . ." Maria got annoyed. "Stop talking like that."

"Take a day off. What's the big deal? No important tests coming up."

"I'm fine!" She was emphatic.

But she wasn't fine. I tried a different approach. "Go to the nurse and—"

"The nurse?"

"Yeah . . . the school nurse."

She laughed and hit my shoulder. "You're in a mood. Should I also be seeing the school purse? How about the school curse?"

I couldn't respond. It was getting easier to take Jace's advice and keep quiet because nothing was making sense. I put the accident recitation on hold.

Maria brightened. "Food would help. I'm starved. Let's get lunch."

"Good idea." The cafeteria was packed. I checked the menu

posted on the walls, and it was macaroni day, hence the hoards. "I'm going to just grab a candy bar from the vends."

Maria considered her options. "Not in the mood for sugar. I think I'll brave the crowds."

"You think?"

"I'm willing if you are, babe."

"Then let's do it." I mock-dived into the thick swarm of teenagers. Maria laughed, then disappeared into the teenage mob. A second later, I regretted my decision not to go with a candy bar.

"Ow!" I complained. "Come on, now!" Within a few moments, my toes had been stepped on, my hair had been ripped on someone's button or pin, and my arms had been smacked in three different places. Plus I was nowhere near the front of the line. I was sandwiched by Ellen Garten in front and Mr. Addison, my history teacher, in back. Today he was wearing a golfer's cap.

"Hello there, Hutchenson."

"Hi, Mr. Addison. Would you like to go ahead of me?"

He gave me the famous "Addison smile"—lopsided with just a touch of irony. "That wouldn't be very democratic."

"I never knew Buchanan was a democracy."

"True enough, Hutchenson. I thank you for your offer, but I'm willing to suffer the slings and arrows with the plebes. Are you all set for the upcoming field trip?"

My heart started racing . . . field trip . . . nightmares.

". . . all right?" he asked.

Mr. Addison was talking to me. "Yes, sir, I'm fine." But I wasn't. "I think I'm just hungry. Are you sure you don't want to go ahead? It's taking a long time." I backed away. "I insist."

My teacher was staring at me. "Okay. Thank you, Kaida." Another smile, but this one was kindly. "Eat a good lunch, all right?"

I nodded. After a fifteen-minute Herculean struggle, I obtained a minuscule dollop of macaroni in a tiny bowl with a side of potato salad. I exited the line, dreaming of those few cheesy bites of macaroni, they'd be so glorious, so victorious, so—

"Gah!" I shouted as a large guy bumped into me.

My hard-fought-for and well-earned macaroni lay on the floor.

And I had almost made it to my table.

"Clean that up!" a prissy girl shouted from her table. Her glossy hair was slicked back into a high ponytail, the kind that always gives me headaches. Her large wet eyes grew in diameter and she shook her head impatiently. "Do it before someone friggin' slips!"

"Since when are you so concerned about public welfare?" I snapped back.

But it seemed like she genuinely was. She left her table and reappeared a minute later with a bunch of paper towels, scrubbing at my pathetic floor-tainted macaroni. "It's people like you!" she snarled at me.

"I was going to clean it up," I explained. "You were just too quick for me."

"Yeah, right!"

I didn't know why she was so angry. I was still staring at the shiny spot on the floor when someone tapped my shoulder. I snapped out of my daze.

"I do believe it's our second encounter."

I looked up—way up—trying to place the face to the smooth voice. The boy was half smiling, with a trace of a five o'clock shadow.

I liked him already.

"You bumped into me yesterday morning," he stated with unabashed bluntness.

I sucked in air. *"Au contraire, mon frère, you* bumped into *me."*

"Is that so?" He shook his head, and bluish black waves undulated. I suspected he dyed his hair—a kind of lame thing for a guy to do—but it didn't matter because the color looked so good on him. He folded his arms across his chest. "I disagree with that assessment. But I do admit that I bumped into you just now. Think of it as revenge."

"Or karma."

"Same thing, different forces." He looked at the shiny spot. "I am sorry about the macaroni, though. Do you want me to get you another one?" he asked.

"Nah, I'm all right. It's still too crowded."

"We can share. I've got enough for two. I even have two forks." When I hesitated, he said, "Offer only goes once."

I held out my hands like a scale, each palm on either side of me. I tipped one up and the other down, then reversed it. "I think I'll take advantage and say yes."

We sat at a cafeteria table occupied by three people who were hunched over textbooks, concentrating on AP calculus. I spotted Maria a few tables away, and she regarded me with an expression that was both confused and entertained.

He handed me a fork and we dug into the gooey mess. It was perfect. As soon as it hit my mouth, I started feeling better. Food was normal and ordinary. After the last couple of days, normal and ordinary were good. After studying him, I decided he might have looked vaguely familiar. How someone that cute could have escaped my notice was puzzling. "So," I began, "had we ever met before yesterday's collision?"

The AP study group gave us dirty looks and left en masse for another table. He laughed. "Is it my breath?"

"Grinds . . . don't you love them?"

"Some people just have to work harder than others." He shoveled macaroni into his mouth, but at least he chewed with his mouth closed. "We've never met because I just got here. I'm trying out the school for a couple of weeks. I got into Fairfield Prep on scholarship, but I wanted to see how I liked the public school. Hey, are you friends with Jenna Michaels?"

73

"No, not at all. Why would you think that?"

"Because she dyes her hair wild colors, too."

"Jenna has blue hair," I pointed out. "I have purple. Purple-ish."

"What's your real hair color?"

"What does it matter?"

"Just making conversation."

"It would help if I knew your name."

"Ozzy."

"Like the rock star?"

"If you want to associate me with him, that's cool."

There was an overly long silence. "Are you going to ask my name?"

Ozzy had dark green eyes, not mint green like mine. "I would love to know your name." He smiled impishly. "Speak to me of it, Juliet."

"Just for that, now you'll have to guess, Rumpelstiltskin." I prompted him with a wave of my hand.

"It's either very unique or ridiculously ordinary. And by the way, it wasn't Rumpelstiltskin who did the guessing, it was the mother of the child." Before I could zing him a nasty retort, he said, "Your name is either common like Ashley or quirky like Mocha or Rose. Give me a hint . . . like the country of origin?"

"Good call, Ozzy. My name is Japanese."

"Japanese?" He threw his head back. "You're joking, right?"

"Not at all."

He took in my contradictory appearance: freckles with purple hair and a long face on a small body. "Yoshi?"

"Never heard of it."

"Megumu?"

"Haven't heard of that one, either." I looked up at the ceiling. The perforations on the tiles reminded me of sky constellations on crack. "Kaida."

"Katie?"

"Kai-da." My body filled with warmth when I said my own name. It was also filling with heat from those gorgeous eyes. Where had he been keeping himself? I hid behind a forkful of macaroni before I could embarrass myself further and I ate a few bites. Then I decided to change the subject. "Were the phones out yesterday?"

"I don't believe so. Why?"

"I saw a car crash. I called nine-one-one, but no one answered."

We sat still, staring at each other. His face had suddenly become grave and even a little scared. I tried out a smile, but his expression remained stiff. I felt very stupid and random.

"So I think I'd better go." I shot out of my chair and ran through the crowds of the cafeteria. Running away from the most beautiful boy I'd ever seen.

He could've called after me. And maybe he even did. But I couldn't be sure, so it would have been stupid to turn back.

"Why am I so socially awkward?" I plunked myself down in a chair next to Maria.

Her brown eyes narrowed as they bored into mine. "Who was that?"

"His name is Ozzy." I answered with feigned disinterest, stealing the cinnamon bun that she had gotten from the vending machine.

"Oh, don't be so nonchalant." She grabbed her pastry back. "He's hot!"

"I didn't notice."

"Right, and I don't have twelve toes."

This was true. Maria was extremely proud of her twelve toes. She had the nicest shoes of anyone on the planet because they had to be custom-made. "I really shouldn't go around advertising that." A nervous laugh. "Don't want too many people thinking I'm a freak."

"And I shouldn't have purple hair, but it is what it is."

"Oz-zy!" She pronounced the name like her whole tongue had been dunked in honey. "Ozzy is quite fetching."

"That's enough out of you," I said. "He just got here. He's trying out Buchanan for a couple of weeks. I hope he likes it."

"Taken, are we?" She raised an eyebrow and sipped her root beer.

"You *have* a boyfriend!" I said this without knowing whether my statement was legitimate. Maria went through guys like Suzanne went through diapers—daily and not very cleanly. "So really, you think he's cute?"

"I think he's, h-h-h . . ." She sneezed and wiped her nose on her sweater.

"You sound like someone stuck Mount Kilimanjaro up your nose," I remarked.

"Yeah, well," she mumbled in a nasty tone.

"Why the bitterness?"

"You know why!" she shot back in an undertone.

I shrugged. "Just take a sick day—"

"Stop talking smack. Change the subject, Kaida. You're not being funny now."

And just then I saw Ozzy walk by. His mossy eyes zeroed in on Maria and me. They finally settled on my face.

"Hey." Maria smiled at him. "How goes it?"

"Not bad." He gave us a half smile and waved. Then he walked away, turning back once more to look at me.

Just me!

Stifling a smile, I stood up. "I've got to go to my locker before next period."

"More like chasing after your prey." Maria held my arm. "Don't be so obvious."

"I'm not running after him, I really do have to—" We heard a hacking noise and both of us turned around.

One of the girls from the AP calculus group had turned bright red. Her friends were hitting her back.

"Oh, my God!" I said to Maria. "She's choking!"

"I know," Maria whispered.

It seemed like the entire cafeteria was mesmerized by some invisible force. "Isn't anyone going to *do* something?"

But nobody did. Even Maria just continued to stare. Then out of the blue, Zeke Anderson went up to her and performed a Heimlich. A piece of macaroni came flying out of her mouth, and the poor girl was suddenly able to breathe. But instead of thanking him, one of the big guys from the AP group glared at Zeke. The boy was over six feet tall and played football.

"What the hell are you doing, Anderson?" He pushed Zeke in the chest. "Getting in my girl's face."

"I was trying to help—"

"Stay away from her!" Another push. "You hear me?"

Zeke blushed and backed away. "I hear you." He turned around and we locked eyes.

I'm sure that his astounded expression mirrored my own.

8

I woke up shaky and disconcerted and I did lousy on a science quiz that afternoon. I knew what was wrong and I knew I had to do something about it. Perched atop a washing machine, locked in the laundry room, I did what I should have done yesterday. Now, after the choking incident, I knew I didn't have a choice.

There was a cordless phone in my hand and a wrinkled piece of paper on my lap.

Zeke Anderson
47893 Canyonette Drive
Home number . . .

I was wearing my favorite oversized sweatshirt and pajama pants. Such sloth at five in the afternoon was one of my few indulgences. The washing machine below me hummed a very dull tune.

"Okay." I found it calming to talk to myself. I always listened and I rarely talked back. "Here goes."

I hit the numbers on the phone. As it continued to ring and ring, I started praying for the wrong number.

"Hello?" a voice answered on the other end.

"Is Zeke Anderson available?" I muttered in haste.

"Speaking." He sounded out of breath.

"Did you just run the mile or something?"

"Who is this?"

The clothes below me swirled and rotated. "It's, um, Kaida."

There was a pause.

"One sec." In the background, I heard people talking and immediately recognized the whiny voice of Leslie Barker. Then I heard a door close behind him. "Kaida Hutchenson?"

"Yeah. Do you know any other Kaida?"

"What's up?"

"I think you need to come over." I didn't know how else to initiate a meeting with Zeke Anderson.

"I feel the need to remind you I have a girlfriend." He chuckled.

My face heated up. "Yeah, everyone and the king of Spain

knows that. Look. Do you want to come over or not?"

If he said yes, I would know that I wasn't nuts. If he said no, I'd say never mind and hang up and that would be that. I wouldn't ever think about it again. I heard Zeke inhale sharply. "I think I get it. You live on Agatha, right?"

"Yes, I'm on Agatha. It's around six miles from your place." Five and a half, actually. I had MapQuested the route already.

"Okay. Ordinarily, I'd have Leslie take me, but that's not a good idea right now. I'll take the bus."

I forgot Leslie was old for our grade and already had her driver's license—the perks of having a plus-one. "Why can't Leslie take you?"

"Because she's already pissed at me because she thought I was trying to put a move on Moose's girl."

"The one who was choking?"

"Yeah."

"That's ridiculous."

"We'll talk later," Zeke said. *"Au revoir, mon amie."*

He hung up. My grandfather was French and I was semi-fluent as well as the vice president of the French Club. Was Zeke alluding to this? I wondered if he'd been researching me in the Buchanan directory.

I'd definitely researched Zeke last night. I had already known—pre-stalking—that he was on the swim team and had some prestige by being the cocaptain of the debate team.

In my freshman yearbook, I saw a ton of pictures of him with Emory Dallard, last year's debate team captain, who had headed off to Columbia University.

Buchanan High's yearbook had this page called Krazy Kapshuns. I didn't know why it was spelled so ridiculously. I think the whole idea was birthed in the '60s or '70s when incorrectly spelling things was cool. Krazy Kapshuns featured photos of students—both normal and silly pictures—with ridiculous captions added onto them. Last year there was a picture of Zeke with Emory, both of them wearing white button-down shirts, mugging for the camera.

The caption above Zeke said, *"Emory, can you PLEASE put me in your suitcase when you go to Columbia?"*

Emory's caption said, *"Sorry, Zeke, but I have a girl-friend."*

I was thinking about the picture because it said something about Zeke and his quest to be cool and popular and to hang with the kids who represented conventional success. He would never agree to meet me unless there was something weird going on.

Hopping down, I took the clothes out of the washing machine and shoved them into the dryer. I switched from sitting atop the washing machine to lying across both machines. Below me the dryer moved like a beast.

I closed my eyes and got into the swishing rhythm of the moment, the room warm and womblike. I must have drifted off into a fitful sleep. The next thing I heard was footsteps. Zeke ambled into the laundry room with my brother right behind him.

"If you call someone up to come over, please do not sequester yourself in hard-to-find spots." Jace was mad at me. He'd been so upset with me lately, and for the life of me I didn't know why. We usually got along very well.

"Sorry." I sat upright and gave Zeke an apologetic look.

"I figured you'd be in here," Jace went on. "This is where your teenage girl crap goes down."

"So if you knew where I'd be, why are you so pissed off?"

"Don't close the door, Kaida. You know the rules."

"He's just here for a science project."

Jace laughed in my face. "Yo, ho, ho, and a bottle of friggin' rum."

"My periodic table or yours?" Zeke croaked out. Quite bravely, I decided.

"Chemistry was never my subject." Jace shrugged. "You two bore me. Have fun with the eeons or whatever."

"Ions," Zeke corrected. Although he was trying to feign casualness, his baby blues were deadly serious. He wore jeans, a polo shirt, and moccasins and looked preppy neat. He waited until Jace was far away, then said, "We're not really here for chem, unless you have a different agenda."

"No, I think we both know why I called you." I felt a lump in my throat. Usually that meant I was happy, sad, or coming

83

down with a cold. But this lump was from raw nerves. For the past few days, my stomach had been producing gallons of acid. "Before I go on, I think there's someone else who should be here."

Zeke was mute, so I took the initiative.

"On the count of three, say his or her name, okay? But whisper. Jace has been crabby."

"Got it."

"One-two-three."

"Joy," we said in unison.

"W-wow," I stuttered. It was comforting yet terrifying to know we were thinking similarly. "Do you want to call her?"

"You have the phone, Hutchenson. You do it."

Just because we had an understanding didn't mean I liked him any better.

Joy said she'd be over in ten minutes.

I had also researched Joy in the yearbook. She had two sad photographs in the Buchanan annual. One was the standard black-and-white photo that everyone got, and there she looked incredibly miserable. The bags under her eyes were distinguishable even in the tiny picture, and her hair was pulled back. Apparently she had had a lip ring last year, but she didn't have one now. One club was listed under her extracurriculars: Mathletes.

The other picture of Joy was with a spiky-haired guy with his arm around her. I recognized him as a senior from last year who had been in French Club with me. He spoke fluently with a perfect Parisian accent. I also knew he, in stereotypical French fashion, smoked like a fiend. I had taken one puff of a Galois once and decided I could never be 100 percent French.

When she showed up, Joy was wearing a loose zip-up hoodie and sweatpants. "I think I know why you called me down." She was clutching her arm. "At least, I think I might know . . . but maybe I don't know."

No one spoke. It was my house. That made me in charge. *Move it along, Kaida.*

"We're here because we sure as hell aren't in Kansas anymore."

"Got that right, Dorothy." Zeke twisted his lips into a crooked smile.

Joy said, "I smoked in the school halls yesterday." She was still cradling her arm. "Mrs. Mimms gave me a light."

"Kaida and I saw a car crash. We called nine-one-one, but there was no answer. No paramedics . . . no firefighters. Just some weird guys in white who took the body away."

"It's called the cleanup crew," I said. "That's what my brother called them, at least."

"I told Leslie about it." Zeke paced in front of us. "She looked at me like I was crazy . . . no, not crazy. Like okay, so what's the big deal? Then she said, 'It's not good, but it happens. Be happy it didn't happen to you.' Leslie is not much for emotions, but this was . . . crazy!"

"Same with my brother," I told him. "The most he said

was that it was gross. Not a word about that poor man . . ." My eyes watered. "Maybe if he would have seen it himself . . ."

"Something's missing here," Joy finished in a hollow voice.

"Really missing!" Zeke shook his head. "Like Mr. Darquest says in chem, let's review the evidence."

"But in a private place." I hopped off the dryer. "Follow me."

And they did—across the house and up the stairs, turning left into my tiny sanctuary. My space had undergone changes depending on my whims. It started when I was seven. I went through a color-on-walls phase. I had filled my room with doodles—stick figures, houses with oversized trees, lots of scribbling. It all got painted away when I went through my next phase: the coffee-shop décor with a red-checked bedspread and white shelves with a soda counter for a desk. That lasted until about a year ago when I painted my room orange. Now my space was just messy with posters and pictures, a silver lamé bedspread, and a boring desk.

I sat on my white tile floor left over from the coffee-shop days, and Joy sat next to me. Zeke closed my door and sat in the chair by my junk-covered desk.

"No nine-one-one, no smoking prohibition." Zeke ticked down a finger at each fact. "And Moose thinks I'm hitting on his girl when I successfully did a Heimlich on her. I *saved* her life, and no one said a word! All I got was a bruise on my chest!"

"What's going on?" Joy asked. After Zeke explained the

cafeteria incident to her, she pulled out a pack of Marlboros and said, "Anarchist society?"

"Open the window if you're going to do that," I told her. "And whisper."

"Why?" Joy's voice was reptilian dry. "No one cares anymore. It sure isn't illegal to buy them if you're under eighteen. I got these at the supermarket."

"Legal or not, I don't want to breathe in your smoke," I snapped. "We have a baby, for God's sakes!"

"Sorry, Kaida, I didn't know." Joy jumped up to open my window before lighting a thin, white cigarette.

"Maybe it's not bad for you anymore," Zeke proposed. "Maybe that's what it is. Tobacco doesn't cause cancer."

"So maybe there's no such thing as cancer," Joy said.

"Or no such thing as disease."

"That can't be it," I said as I played with the ends of my hair.

Joy blew out a ribbon of smoke. "Why not?"

"Maria was coughing this morning. She was sick, although she didn't want to admit it. She didn't even know what a nurse was. Or maybe she did and was making fun of me. It's hard to tell with her. There *has* to be disease if she was sick."

Zeke said, "Maybe it's not the same kind of disease. Maybe bad things don't happen. Like maybe . . . choking isn't so bad . . . or something."

"She was beet red, Zeke. It looked pretty serious to me." I paused. "Can we talk about Carlsbad for a minute?"

"The upcoming trip," Joy said. "Whoopdy-do."

"Upcoming trip . . ." I repeated. "So I guess you didn't have a weird dream?"

She was silent, but her eyes darted from side to side. It was the most animation I'd ever seen from her. Zeke and I exchanged glances. He said, "I had a weird dream."

"Tell me about it," I said.

"No, you go first."

"I dreamed we were on our way to Carlsbad and we were in a car crash—"

"Oh, God!" Joy started to cry. "No, no, no!"

"Shhh!" I told her. "My brother will hear you."

Joy clamped her hand over her mouth. Then she spoke in hushed tones. "It can't be real."

"Sure as hell seemed real to me," Zeke whispered. "There was a terrible storm and the three of us went hiding in a cave." He turned to Joy. "You hurt your arm."

"I didn't!" She sobbed without tears. "It's fine!"

"Then why are you clutching it?" Zeke asked her.

"Leave her alone!" I whispered fiercely. "And keep your voice down."

"Sorry. . . ." Zeke turned to Joy. "Sorry."

"We all had the same dream," I said. "I'm sure of it. The good news is that we're probably not crazy. The bad news is something's going on, and we don't know what it is."

"It has to be a dream," Joy said. "Mr. Addison is still alive."

I had no answer to that one, and neither did Zeke.

I said, "The last thing I remember before waking up is falling."

"Me, too," Zeke said. "We got lost in the cave and we were struggling to find our way out. Then we saw light."

"We began running toward an opening," Joy said.

"And then we fell," I said. "But I don't remember hitting the ground."

"I didn't hit the ground," Joy said. "I woke up and my arm was red and sore."

"So where are we?" When no one answered, I said, "Everything's the same, except it isn't. What is it? Like a bizarro world where everything's backwards?"

"Nothing is backwards," Joy said. "Everything's the same except no one will help me with my arm. I told my mom about it and she slapped me." Her eyes grew moist. "She said I was fine. I was really angry at her until I noticed this terrified look in her eyes . . . like I was going to die or something. It scared the living crap out of me. Then I told my boyfriend about it and he got angry at me and told me to shut up." More tears. "He never talks that way to me. I was so mad at him, I told him I never wanted to see him again."

"So how is your arm?" I asked her.

"If I don't move it too much, it's okay. Please don't speak about it. I just want to forget about it, okay?"

"So there *is* disease." My head was throbbing, and an

inferno was raging inside my stomach. "Disease exists, but no one wants to talk about it."

"Wait." Zeke snapped his fingers. "You said Maria was sick. Did she go home early?"

I tossed my hair back. "No."

"That's it!" Zeke cried. "There is disease, but there's no concept of getting sick!"

No one said anything.

Zeke exclaimed, "No one truly understands the meaning of illness."

"She *did* get pissed when I suggested she take a sick day," I added.

Joy shook her head. "No, then she wouldn't have gotten pissed. She'd just be confused. They know what getting sick means. And both my mom and my boyfriend—my ex-boyfriend—knew what being hurt was. They just don't want to acknowledge being sick or hurt. Like getting germs is a death sentence or something."

"That could be," Zeke said. "Leslie was weird when I tried to kiss her last night. And then she looked at me like I was nuts."

"And that's just making out." Joy smashed her cigarette against my windowpane. "I could only imagine what it's like for people who seriously hook up—if you know what I mean."

I knew exactly what she meant. I got up and began to walk

around my room. It was in a state of chaos. My plaid kilt was rumpled on the floor and my underwear drawer was embarrassingly open. Subtly I tried to close it with the side of my body. "So maybe people do understand sick but just don't want to talk about it because there are no cures."

"That could be," Joy said. "After my mom slapped me . . . I went into the kitchen cupboard to look for Advil. That's where we keep it—or used to keep it. It was gone. Maybe we just ran out, but I wasn't about to ask my mom about it."

"It could be that there's no pills here. My medicine cabinet was missing my stuff, too." I glanced at my bulletin board. On it were pictures of Maria and me, Iggy and Stephen. There was also a photo from last year in the hospital when Suzanne had just been born. It was of my whole family and one of my favorites. The photo was right in the middle—

My mouth dropped open.

"Kaida, are you all right?" Joy asked.

I whipped my head around. I was panting.

"Sit down," Zeke told me. "You're white."

"More like gray." Joy pulled out another cigarette and lit it. "Are you okay?"

I didn't answer her. "My photo!" I smacked the wall. "It's gone!"

Not really *physically* gone, but it had morphed. We were no longer at the hospital, but at my grandmother's house. I just stared and stared and stared. "I think I finally get this."

"What?" Zeke said. "Clue us in."

"No medicine, no hospitals, no nurses, and no doctors."

We sat in dazed silence.

"People do understand sick." I shivered. "They just don't understand better."

9

It was a defining moment.

"People get sick," I whispered. "They don't understand how to *stop* being sick."

Zeke was appalled. "How could you have a society with flat screens, email, computers, cell phones, and fax machines but no medicine?"

"Then come up with something better." I turned away from my bulletin board and faced the two of them. Zeke was too big for my chair. Joy didn't seem at ease with her cigarette. It was as if she had stolen it from her mother's dresser drawer—a kid in Mommy's makeup.

I took the cigarette from Joy's fingers, crushed it under my foot, and threw it out of the window. "If there's no such thing as better, you don't need to have crap in your lungs."

"I . . ." Joy looked down. "I don't know what to say."

I turned to look at Zeke. "You just coughed!"

"I did?"

"Yeah, you did," Joy confirmed.

I told him, "Cough again tonight. Ask your mom for a cough drop! She probably won't even know what it is. That's why Moose thought you were coming on to his girlfriend. There's no such thing as a Heimlich maneuver."

"Kaida, calm down," Joy said.

I was talking too loud. I took two yoga breaths and tried to calm my thumping heart. "You're both in denial!"

I felt the tears come.

Gah!

I hate crying in front of other people. I sat on my bed, pulling my knees to my chin. My head felt safe in the space between my knees: nice and dark.

"No one's in denial," Zeke said in hushed tones. "At least, I'm not. I'm just utterly confused. Like we're here and everything's the same, except it's not the same. Like we're in some kind of facsimile of our world . . ." His voice broke.

I knew it was bad when a boy like Zeke got choked up.

Joy's voice was also shaky. "What's going on?"

"I have no idea, but something has radically changed." I told them about how the hospital where my sister was born had disappeared from the picture on my bulletin board.

Zeke put his hand over his mouth. "This is too weird. I need to think about this."

"And I need to get home," Joy said. "My mother . . . she doesn't care about me smoking, but she's suddenly become a bug on time."

I looked up. "Take care of the arm. I'll try to find some Advil."

"Yeah, me too," Zeke said. "I'll hunt around."

"We need to agree not to talk to anyone about it," Joy said. "No one."

We all nodded.

Joy said, "I'm beginning to believe Kaida . . . that medicine doesn't exist."

"Or hospitals or doctors," I said. "It's either that or I'm going mad."

"Then I'm going crazy, too," Zeke said. "I have to go as well."

But no one moved.

Zeke said, "It's going to look really weird if we all suddenly hang out together when we never did before the accide . . . before the dream."

"I agree," I said. "We'll keep a low profile. We shouldn't hang out. But maybe can meet for a few minutes at lunch and talk about it tomorrow."

They both nodded. I dried my eyes and tried to appear as normal as possible. I walked them to my door and closed it softly after they left. Then I ran back to my room, stuffed my face into my pillow, and silently cried. But I wasn't alone for long.

"Knock, knock," Jace called from outside.

"Screw you," I told him.

He opened my door anyway. When he saw my red eyes, he swallowed dryly. "You okay?"

"I'm fine. I'm having a bad day."

"Sorry about that." He sat beside me on my bed and twisted my earlobe. I have the type of earlobes that connect directly into my head, hence earning me the loving name "Lobeless." Jace had called me that since I was ten. He didn't twist it hard, but I found it irritating.

"Ow." I swatted his hand away. "Something is wrong."

"I'll say, Lobeless. I'm in your room of my own free will."

"Don't call me that. I'm not in the mood."

Jace rubbed his hands together. "It's about what happened. You know, the thing with the car and the guys in white . . ."

I hadn't even told him about the choking incident. I wanted to tell him about that as well but then thought better of it.

Jace's eyes swept across my room. "Your questioning about the accident is not acceptable. You know that."

I hadn't known that, but I was starting to learn. "Nothing is making sense."

He nodded. "You're asking about things that you know can't be answered. I once felt the same as you did. Confused. Do you know what I did?"

"Eat?"

"Well, yeah, I did that, too." He looked around my room again. "When I had those kinds of questions and I didn't want to ask anyone about them because . . . well, you know how parents are."

"I'm figuring that out as we speak."

"Anyway, when I had questions, I went to the library."

"Jace, I do not need one of those 'you and your body' books—"

"Stop, stop, stop!" He exhaled again. "You're not going to get the kind of answers you want. You'll never get exactly what you want. But there are people out there . . . who have thought about these things . . . things that we're not supposed to think about."

"But why aren't we supposed to think about them?"

"Because spills are dangerous, bad, and if you use them and something happens, you'll be accused of murder. You know that. Everyone knows that. Spills kill."

I didn't understand a word he was saying. *"Spills?"*

He looked around as if we were being videotaped. "Let me say that I found that out the hard way and nearly got us all arrested."

"Arrested?"

"It was two years ago during the summer, when they sent you away to Aunt Jen and Uncle Len for a couple of weeks."

"Ugh. That was horrible!"

"They didn't want you around, just in case. That's why I

97

got so pissed off when you started asking questions." He pulled my earlobes again. "You remind me of me. So if you're going to ask questions, make sure you go through the proper channels. You can't do it unannounced."

"What are you talking about?"

"The archives."

"The what?"

"I was told that there are interesting things down there. But you have to be careful, okay?" He reached into his pocket, fished out a crumpled ID, and gave it to me. His face looked very emotional. "I saved this."

"Who is . . ." I read the ID. "Who's Erin White?"

"A girl I once knew who doesn't exist anymore."

"What are you *talking* about?"

He looked away, then back at me. "If you go to the library and find the archives, this may work. Tell whoever is in charge that you're doing a college research paper for Iona Boyd."

"College? I'm not even sixteen."

"Just do it." He walked out of my room but popped his head back in a few seconds later to say, "And if you want to look older, wear makeup."

"I do!" I shouted.

But he was long gone.

I rubbed my right eye, and a splotch of black leaked onto my hand.

Aha.

Proof!

* * *

Zeke and Joy were eating lunch together. They were leaning their heads inward as if they were having a very private conversation. Joy's silky hair was draped over one side of her face and one of her slim hands was supporting her head, a silver ring on her pinky finger. She was nodding, looking grave and much older than fourteen.

Much older than eighteen, actually, and that was good. Maybe she could convince whoever needed to be convinced that she was in college and doing a research paper.

Zeke was rubbing his temples in concentrated frustration.

"Hi." I dropped my tray onto their table and my apple bounced and fell off.

"Kaida!" Joy cleared her throat. She sat up. Zeke put on a fake grin.

"Look, I'm going to be honest," I said as I sat down. "Either we believe the dream wasn't a dream or we don't. We can't waste time arguing about it."

They looked at each other. Zeke's eyes reminded me of a clear lake—without any fish swimming in it, of course. "We were just talking about this," he began. "It's not about believing, Kaida, it's about whether it's smart to believe whether it happened or not."

I reached for my tray, but Joy stopped me.

"Hold on for a moment, okay?" Joy whispered. "I'm the one with the arm, so quit being a baby."

I nodded. I was acting pretty infantile. Not getting my

way and having a temper tantrum. "I'm moving forward. If you two want to be in on this, then fine. We'll move forward together. Because what we're doing . . . what we've been saying . . . people are talking. We've got to be careful if we continue."

They both nodded.

Zeke said, "So what's next?"

Joy said, "Your theory, Kaida, is definitely a possibility. But don't you think we should do a little more research before we start going all Nancy Drew?"

"Yes, and that's exactly why I'm here. I have an idea."

Zeke and Joy leaned in close. I felt like a conspirator involved in something very dangerous. My parents always call me "rebel without a cause." Now I had a legitimate cause, and instead of making me feel special, it only made me scared. "My brother and I were talking last night." I dug my spoon into a cup of vanilla yogurt. "He was really nervous . . . saying that I was asking questions that can't be answered."

"We really need to stop asking other people questions," Zeke said.

"No, what we really need is to find some answers," I told him. "But carefully . . . really carefully."

The two of them agreed.

I took a deep breath and let it out. "He said to check in the archives at the library."

"What archives?" Joy asked. She tucked her hair behind her ears.

"I don't know. I've never been there. But he did say that I might find answers, or at least find people who have asked the questions we're asking. The trouble is you have to get permission to get into them."

Zeke asked, "What kind of permission?"

"I'm not sure. He gave me this ID card and told me to use it if I find the archives. The girl looks a little like me, so maybe that's a good idea. He also said my cover story . . . our cover story . . . should be that we're in college and doing a research paper with a woman named Iona Boyd. He also told me to wear makeup so I look older and more believable." I shrugged and swallowed my yogurt. "Or maybe he just thinks I look ugly."

My attempt at levity fell flat.

Zeke said, "How do we get permission to use the archives?"

"I haven't the faintest idea. And he made it sound like asking for permission was a dangerous thing."

"Dangerous in what way?" Joy wanted to know.

"He wasn't specific." I fudged on this one. I wasn't about to tell them that he almost got my entire family arrested and about how using "spills" was like committing murder. Or maybe he was exaggerating.

I was in a quandary. I wanted to warn them but not scare them off. But the more I thought about it, the more I concluded that it was morally wrong not to come clean. Just because I was going on a crusade didn't mean I had the right to drag others into my quest.

"My brother made it sound like doing this kind of research could potentially get us into deep, deep trouble. Like really bad trouble. Like being arrested."

"For *what*?" Joy asked.

"I don't *know*! That's the problem." I looked at their anxious faces. "But we need to find out. *I* need to find out. So if anyone wants to back away, now's your chance."

No response. I gave it another shot.

"Honestly, from what he told me, it sounded like we could all get arrested for *murder*."

"For doing *research*?" Zeke was skeptical.

"It's insane, but nothing surprises me anymore."

"I'm with Kaida," Joy said. "We're operating under different rules. The trouble is we don't know what they are."

"In or out?" I said.

"In," Zeke and Joy said at the same time.

"So we'll meet on Saturday at Hawthorne Library . . . say, eleven o'clock?"

"We have to wait until Saturday?" Zeke said.

"I don't know about you, but I'd rather commit an entire day to this, not have to squeeze it in as an after-school project."

"I agree," Joy said.

I realized that Joy was holding her arm. She did it all the time now. "So Saturday at eleven?"

"See you then," Zeke said.

"And maybe in the meantime, we should act like before . . . like not hang around one another?"

"Just when I was beginning to think you were tolerable," Zeke told me. "Whatever you want, Hutchenson, you seem to have elected yourself the boss."

Just at that moment, Leslie Barker and a friend who seemed to be shadowing her passed us and knocked over an empty seat at our table.

"The wife's not happy?" I asked the Zekemeister.

"No." Zeke rubbed his forehead. He seemed to have aged since last night. I suppose we all did. "She broke up with me this morning."

"Can I ask why?"

He looked me square in the eye. "Two reasons. One, she didn't like the questions I was asking her. And two, she didn't like my new friends. So if you're worried about us hanging together, I wouldn't be concerned. It looks like we've been made."

I felt sheepish. "I'm sorry."

Joy said, "We'll sink or swim together."

Zeke smiled. "No worries. I'm a good enough swimmer for the three of us."

Boys and their bravado. Joy said, "Hey, Anderson, now that we're 'made' and you're not so busy, how about helping me with chemistry? I didn't do my homework."

"Nothing better to do."

"My book's in my locker."

Zeke stood up. "Might as well be useful to someone. Let's go."

They left, and I smiled to myself.

I hadn't seen that one coming.

Attraction works in strange ways.

10

The Nathaniel Hawthorne Library was housed in an old-fashioned building made of white stucco with marble fluted columns in front and a big peaked roof. People referred to it as the White House, and although that was an exaggeration, it was the closest thing we had to grand architecture. The interior was august, with high ceilings and a marble-tiled floor that clacked against high-heeled shoes. Lucky for us, we were wearing our Vans.

We had all tried to dress up to look a little older and a little more professional. Joy wore a black skirt and dark sweater. I was in my orchestra uniform—a black skirt and a white blouse. Zeke had put on a polo shirt and slacks.

There were shelves upon shelves filled with books, CDs, DVDs, and a lot of dust. No one knew where to start. Zeke whispered, "How do we do this?"

"I don't know," I answered. "Jace said the archives are here, but it wouldn't be smart to ask where they are."

"So how are we supposed to find them?"

"Again, I don't know." I let out a sigh. "Maybe we should just start looking around?"

We were all whispering. Joy coughed and dug into her purse, extracting a cigarette. When she saw disapproval in our eyes, she said, "I see at least three people here who're smoking."

"That may be," Zeke said softly, "but honestly, *now?*"

"I'm just nervous." She threw the cigarette back into her purse.

It might have been my imagination, but I sensed that people were starting to stare at us. Was there something about our expressions that made us stand out? I picked up a random book and began to page through it, trying to look nonchalant.

"What are you doing?" Zeke whispered.

"Trying to fit in," I answered.

Zeke got it and so did Joy. They picked books from the shelves and started doing the same thing. Still looking at the book in front of me, I whispered, "The archives can't be in the main section. Let's try the basement."

"I didn't know the library had a basement." Zeke had picked up a botanical book on orchids.

"Could be it doesn't." I put down the book. "The building has more than one story. Let's find the stairwell."

We put our books back on the shelves and began to hunt for the stairs in earnest, carefully opening doors, hoping that one would lead somewhere. It took another five minutes, but Joy struck gold.

"It goes down here," she whispered to Zeke, who, in turn, waved me over.

We all carefully slipped behind the door, and when it closed, we heard a click.

Zeke tried the door. "Now we're locked in."

I looked at the descending steps. "So that means we have nowhere to go but down." I took in a deep breath and let it out. "We've been down unknown roads before." Everyone knew what I was referring to. "We got out of that and we'll get out of this." My face felt hot, but I tried to show confidence. I led the way.

Down one flight.

Down two flights.

To another door.

"If this is locked, what do we do?" Joy asked.

"We bang," Zeke answered. He slowly began turning the knob.

This one opened.

The room was not much more than an average-sized office.

A man in his early thirties with soft blond curls and a dusty mustache sat at the front desk. Next to him a beautiful Indian woman was on the phone. She looked exotic, with almond eyes and brown skin.

"Excuse me." I approached the desk with trepidation, like when you go into the dentist's chair. Joy and Zeke were behind me. If they had any brains in their heads, their hearts were probably beating as fast as mine was.

"Yes?"

Again I took the lead. "We're here for our college research project in the archives."

His expression turned hard. "Identification?"

I showed him Erin White's card.

He scanned it.

When it clicked, it was all I could do not to shout hurray.

The man waited for Zeke and Joy to get out their IDs.

I forged ahead. "They're with me."

"I don't care if they're with the government." He glared at me. "You don't even look old enough to be in college. Lemme see that card again."

I handed it back to him and scratched my cheek. Foundation rubbed off. I had worn makeup, just as Jace instructed, but there was only so much that disguise could do.

Again the card beeped when it was scanned. This emboldened me. "Can we go?"

"Look here, little one. I'm giving your compadres a chance to get out of here without a black mark. Surely you don't want me writing this up." His stare was fierce. "You're not fooling anyone. Go."

The Indian woman held the phone to her chest for a moment. "Is there a problem?"

"Not so far, but if these two don't leave"—he pointed to Zeke and Joy—"there certainly will be problems."

Joy broke first. "Let's go."

The door from the stairwell opened, providing temporary distraction. When I saw who it was, my mouth dropped open.

"Hi, Mr. Luckman." Ozzy presented his ID and put a packet of papers onto the desk. Then he looked at us with unflappable eyes. "You guys beat me here."

I followed his lead. "That's because you're always late."

"Not so, but I am this time." Ozzy's eyes returned to Mr. Luckman's face. "They're all with me." His posture was casual.

"I can't believe you're back again."

"I know. I'm a pest. That's why we've all been assigned to do the paper together. Less work for me."

The man's face registered pure doubt. He turned to me. "Why didn't you tell me that in the beginning?"

"I told you we were doing a paper."

"But you didn't say you were with Callahan."

"My mistake." I tried out my best "I don't give a damn" shrug.

The man stuck Ozzy's papers under another scanner. The

machine beeped, then the light turned green. He placed the papers in a steel box.

"These two jokers don't have proper ID, Callahan. If you don't start cooperating, I'm going to write you all up."

"Mr. Luckman is all bark but no bite," Ozzy said confidently.

"Don't press it, Callahan." Luckman's eyes narrowed as he regarded my face. "Are you sure you're in college?"

"Next time I'll bring in my grades." I was amazed at my nerve. All that sass I gave my parents was finally paying off.

Mustache Man kept glaring at me. Then he gave me the clipboard. "Sign in."

I began to write my name, starting with a cursive *K*, but then I caught myself. With a shaky hand, I wrote down *Erin White*. Ozzy looked at it but didn't let on.

I said to Joy and Zeke, "I'll meet you upstairs."

"Sure," Zeke said. "I'll write up the outline for the paper while you're getting the information."

Joy nodded. "I'll write up a first draft when you've gotten all that you need."

Both of them looked very happy to dump this on my lap.

"How do we get out?" Zeke asked.

"Same way you got in," Luckman said.

"The door locked behind us."

Luckman rolled his eyes. "When you reach the top, push the wall button and I'll buzz you out. And I'd better not see either one of you again without proper ID."

They nodded and left very quickly.

Ozzy said, "Let's go, Erin. We're under a time crunch." He took me through a door that opened into a blindingly white hallway.

I was thrown off by the starkness and the brightness, but what happened next really shook me up. Ozzy backed me into a corner and whispered, "Who are you?"

"Get out of my face!" I whispered back with anger.

He took a step back. "You sure as hell aren't Erin White. How'd you get her ID? And how the hell did you know the code?"

I stared at him for a long time. "I got the ID from . . . from someone who knew her very well. It was that person who told me about the archives."

"Who was it?"

"None of your damn business."

No one spoke. Then Ozzy sighed. "Sorry." He looked down. "Sorry, that was bad."

I noticed his hands were shaking. Something had riled him terribly. "Who is she? Erin White?" I was still whispering. When Ozzy didn't answer, I said, "And, FYI, I don't know what code you're talking about."

He stood there, breathing hard, trying to calm himself. I was sufficiently composed to notice that he was still good-looking.

He said, "Then why are you here?"

Something clicked in my brain. "How'd you *know* I was here?"

He shrugged, looking up at the ceiling and then back down, focusing his eyes anywhere but on me. He stuck his hands into the pocket of his sweatshirt, which he wore over black jeans.

Then it dawned on me. "Have you been *following* me?"

"Why do you hang out with those guys?" he asked abruptly. "I see you with Maria . . . she's your type. But Zeke and Joy?"

"They're my friends. What do you have against them?"

"Nothing." He looked down. "They just seem like a random group for you."

"What's it your business?"

"It isn't."

"What code are you talking about?"

"God, I have a big mouth!" he whispered to himself. He seemed to be angry, but this time not at me. "Please, please don't tell anyone that I've asked you these questions."

I stared at him for a long time. "I won't. I've learned the hard way that question-asking isn't very welcome nowadays." I exhaled. "Where are these archives?"

His manner was offhand, but his expression was very sober. "What do you want to look up in the archives?"

"Why don't you take me to them and I'll let you know."

His put his hand on my shoulder and smiled with white

112

teeth. "Out here, there's no camera. Once we step inside the door, we've got audio and video everywhere we go. Look like you're flirting with me or something, okay?"

I gave him my most pixyish smile, which wasn't very good.

He laughed. "I know you're acting, but you look good when you smile."

"How do you know about the archives and Erin White?"

"For another time. I'll explain all. *Please* trust me on this."

"You get one chance, Ozzy. Don't blow it."

"I understand." He took my hand. "First we have to go through the stacks. Right this way, mademoiselle."

The door he opened led to another white room. This one had white shelving, a white ceiling, and a white floor. It looked more like a sanitarium than a library.

We passed books on architecture. "What's your favorite genre?" I asked him.

"Oh, I'm all about romantic literature." He wiggled his thick black eyebrows. "I love D. H. Lawrence."

Now I raised my eyebrows. "Really?"

He laughed. "Nah, I'm putting you on. I like comic books and graphic novels."

"I like graphic novels, too."

He nudged me a bit in the ribs. "Don't look so disappointed. In reality, I'm a science nerd."

"You're no more of a science nerd than I am."

He hip-bumped me. "And how do you know that I'm not a science nerd?"

That's right. We have to flirt. I bumped him back. "I have a good feel for these kinds of things."

He gave an evaluating nod. If he wasn't giving anything away, I wouldn't either. We were standing in front of a tremendous door that seemed to be a foot thick. When he opened it, it creaked like something out of a gothic novel. Inside a few people were milling about. I had expected the archives to be an ancient-looking room with smelly leather and cobwebs. I was let down that it was again a bright, white room. Everything here was so utterly sanitized. I felt myself break into a sweat. The white reminded me of the cleanup crew.

A woman with a bundle of red curls was sitting behind a pearlescent plastic desk. Ozzy presented her with his ID, and I gave her my Erin White ID. Even though my ID beeped, she seemed to be assessing us.

Ozzy added, "I was just screened a second ago, Elaine."

"It's not you, Callahan—it's her. She looks about fourteen. Do you have your driver's license?"

"I left it at home," I told her. "He drove."

Elaine picked up the phone and spoke quietly over the line. When she hung up, she said, "Mr. Luckman said just this once." She was looking at me.

"I know I look young for a college student."

"Then bring ID with your birth date."

"Thanks, Elaine," Ozzy told her.

"Don't push my goodwill too far." She checked her watch. "You know the drill. Fifteen minutes."

"You bet." Ozzy led me down a white hallway. There were no bookshelves, only numbered doors.

We cut a turn.

Another hallway.

More sanitarium white.

More doors with numbers on them.

It seemed that we were standing in utter emptiness.

I'm not going to lie—I was creeped out. If Ozzy hadn't been there, I would have been totally lost.

He touched my shoulder and whispered, "We're going to have to talk about this at some point."

I tensed. "When?"

"I dunno." He grinned a little on one side of his mouth. "Soon."

It was all very confusing. Did I dare tell him my theories? He could be one of the bad guys. For all I knew, he might be part of that cleanup crew. Maybe he would sooner throw me in the van than help me.

Ozzy took my hand. "What are you looking for?"

Answers, I thought. But I didn't say anything.

"I know this place pretty well . . . and I think I might know what you want."

That would make one of us, I said to myself.

"Wait here," Ozzy told me. "It'll be faster without you.

Besides, I don't look like I'm about to faint with fright."

"I'm fine," I defended myself.

"You're fine for someone who just got here, but you're not fine for someone who doesn't know what's going on."

"What do you mean *just got here?*"

He evaluated me. "Maybe I'm wrong, but I suspect I'm not. Let me put it this way. There have been the rare others like you, Kaida, but I'm willing to lay money that you're probably the cutest. Wait here and I'll be back." He squeezed my fingers before he let go and disappeared behind one of the doors.

The minutes dragged endlessly. I felt my heart beat and my head throb and I had to concentrate on my breathing to make sure I didn't start panicking. But it was very hard. I was alone. Everything was bathed in white, not a thing to distract my attention.

I kept checking my watch. For every minute that passed, it seemed like ten. Finally, Ozzy reappeared, carrying five or six thick plastic folders.

"Let's go." He started to walk away and I dogged his heels. I wouldn't have followed him had I been sure of my ability to navigate out of the crazy labyrinth.

"Wait a second!" I told him. "My legs are a little shorter than yours."

He slowed. "Sorry."

"How do you know what I'm looking for?"

He turned to me. "You have to get rid of your friends. We'll clue them in later."

"Clue them in to what? You've got to be more forthcoming before I do anything."

"Not here."

"Then don't bring it up."

He didn't answer. I didn't know if we were retracing our steps or not because everything looked the same.

"Who's Iona Boyd?" I asked him.

"A professor. We'll talk about it later."

Somehow he managed to get us back into the white room with the books, and then past the first interrogation desk.

Mr. Luckman took a long time examining the papers that Ozzy had taken. He said, "You can't have this one . . . or this one . . . or this one." He looked up. "You'll need Professor Boyd's prior approval."

"Last time you let me have this one." Ozzy pointed to a folder.

"Well, this time you're out of luck."

"You're the boss. I'll speak to Professor Boyd about it."

"Do that." Luckman handed Ozzy the remaining three folders. "You know the rules, but I have to tell them to you anyway. Papers stay in the special glassine folders. Maximum exposure to light is two minutes or else they start fading. Have them back on Sunday—tomorrow—by nine in the morning. Give me your thumb."

Ozzy complied. Luckman took a thumbprint on a sheet of paper and then placed it into a drawer.

Now it was my turn to be grilled.

Luckman said, "Did you check anything out?"

"No."

"Then why'd you come here?"

"I didn't find what I wanted in fifteen minutes." I smiled. "Next time."

He zeroed in on my face. "Next time, bring your driver's license."

"I promise I will," I told him.

But I knew very well that there wouldn't be a next time.

11

I never thought I'd find the mustiness and the dustiness of upstairs Hawthorne Library so inviting, but it was wonderful to be in a place that was dark and slightly disheveled. It looked like a library and it felt *normal*. It took me awhile to find Zeke and Joy, and when I did they were deep in conversation. Zeke was the first one to notice me. His eyes went from my face to Ozzy's then back to me. They were sitting at a table next to a window that looked out on the park square. In all honesty it appeared the same as it always had—green and lovely and filled with flowers—but now to me everything was skewed and lopsided.

119

"Hey," I said.

"Hey," Joy answered back. "What's going on?"

We sat down. Ozzy said, "We think the best way to do this . . . paper is for Kaida and me to do the research first. We can meet up later. How about at eight tonight?"

"Where? I don't drive," Zeke told him.

"I do," Ozzy said. "So let's meet at your house, Anderson."

"I don't drive, either," Joy said.

"I'll pick up Kaida and then pick you up on the way over, okay?"

"Sounds good." Joy was still wearing a sweater even though it was warm inside. I wondered about the condition of her arm.

"See you all later." Ozzy guided me out of the library.

"Where's your car?" I asked him.

"I said I drive," he told me. "I didn't say I have a car. I've got to go wrangle one up for tonight."

We walked in fresh air and warm sunshine, and it felt remarkably good. A wonderful spring day, but it was hard to enjoy it fully. I felt like I was living in different worlds—one where there were doctors and hospitals, and another where they'd disappeared—or at least had gone into hiding. What other shocking things were in store for me? I didn't want to think about it. "Where are we going?"

"You'll see. Are you hungry?"

"A little."

"What about pizza?"

"Sure." I sighed. "Whatever."

"I could get something else."

"I love pizza, but at the moment, I'm doubtful about my stomach's ability to digest anything."

Ozzy stopped walking and so did I. "Try to relax." A pause. "I know as soon as someone tells you to relax, you can't. But if there's something you can do to just . . ."

I inhaled deeply through my nose to the count of four, and then I exhaled to the count of four.

"Yoga breathing," he said. "That's good." He took out his cell phone. "Anything you like on your pie?"

"Mushrooms and pineapple."

"That is one *strange* combination."

If I had been living in my former life, I would have given him a playful slap or something stupid like that. Now I simply didn't have the energy. "Ozzy, I don't have any cash on me."

He raised his eyebrows. "I'll pay for this one and only charge you ten percent interest." His smile was delicious. He was great to look at, but my mind wasn't on boys. The levity in his face faded. "Anything else, Kaida? I'm getting pasta salad, too."

I shrugged. He placed the order and we walked a few minutes in silence.

"Your mom's not into cooking, huh?" It was a contrast from my mother. She tried to raise us on home-cooked meals, but when Jace reached the wonderful age of teenagerhood, the Chinese take-out era began. Suddenly take-out food tasted far better than the tired dishes that Mom cooked over and over. But that was just us. Whenever we had company for dinner, our friends would rave about Mom's culinary skills.

We walked a little bit more.

I once read about this neurological phenomenon that allowed the gifted few to see music in colors. I often felt that I had the opposite wiring, that I saw colors as music. If the surroundings and the sidewalks were music genres, in this area of town they would be opera. The environs were loud and dramatic with bold graffiti markings, colors, and designs.

Without emotion, Ozzy said, "My mom's sick."

All the blood in my body traveled to my cheeks. I said nothing and glanced at him. His eyes were cast downward, definitely not in the moment. I touched his arm and he gave me a glazed smile. But then I realized something that overrode my embarrassment.

"You said the word," I offered quietly.

We stopped walking. We had entered a residential area with small, clean bungalow houses lined up like soldiers.

"What word?" he asked.

"*Sick.*" By now, I knew enough to whisper. "You said the word *sick*. You and Zeke and Joy are the only people who have said that word."

Sometimes when you're in a situation that you know is important, you take note of all the details around you without even realizing it. Twisting my index finger into one of my pig-tails, I decided I needed a haircut really, really badly. I saw that the sky was the faintest blue, like a blue not bothering to be blue. Ozzy had freckles and was wearing Keds. And I could hear utensils clattering in the background, so someone must have been eating lunch.

"I knew it!" His smile was ever so faint. "I knew it from the beginning . . . when you were talking to Maria, telling her to take a sick day off."

"Why were you eavesdropping on our conversation?"

He looked around him. "Let's go to my house." He picked up the pace and I followed him. We walked for another two blocks until Ozzy bounced up three steps onto a stoop of a little yellow house with white trim. The place was pretty and cozy but was more compact than my own home. This area was not as expensive as where I lived and a lot less expensive than where Zeke's house was.

"Home sweet home." Ozzy turned a key into the door and twisted the knob for a few seconds until the door finally opened.

When you step into a teenager's room, you can clearly tell it's a teenager's room. The floor is usually littered with socks, magazines, and food wrappers. There are posters on the walls, and the whole place smells a little stale.

That was Ozzy's *living room*. The entire house looked like Hurricane Hormone. It put Jace's room to shame.

I could only imagine his bedroom.

"My mother has been sick for a while." He pushed some papers onto the floor and sat on a couch that looked so soft it might have dissolved underneath his weight. "We have to be quiet. She's sleeping."

I sat down next to him and rested my elbows on my knees.

His voice was sad. "This place is a dump. Sorry."

I smiled a little. "Hey, you should see my room before my mother makes me clean it."

"I should take better care of things."

"You can't do everything. Does your father live with you?"

"He's dead."

That was positively the last time I was going to open my mouth.

He drummed his fingers on his thigh and bit his lower lip. "When Mom first got sick, I was twelve." He paused. "Let me rephrase that. When I was twelve, Mom got really sick. It wasn't her first time being sick, because everyone gets sick more than once, right?"

I nodded hesitantly.

"I mean, everyone knows what sick is, but no one will do anything about it."

"But *why*?"

"Why?"

"Yes, *why*. *Why* don't you do anything about it?"

He evaluated my addled expression. "You know. Darwinism: The weak die out, leaving the strong to live and propagate."

"Ozzy, that explains evolution. It has nothing to do with our day-to-day living as human beings."

He stared at me as if I was from another planet. And perhaps I was. I certainly wasn't in a familiar place and it was getting stranger day by day. I felt muddled—as if I was having a very realistic dream that I couldn't wake up from. "Ozzy, I'm confused. Explain it to me. Like I was just *dropped* onto the face of the earth."

"Okay . . ." He drummed his fingers. "Okay, I will."

"Good."

"There's this fear," he whispered. "This pervasive fear . . . that if you tamper with the order of things . . . it's like we are all made a certain way . . . given a certain time . . . and that's it. You don't screw around with nature."

This definitely was not the world *I* came from, but I was too wary to confide in him. As far as I knew, I could be entering headlong into a trap. Until I understood the parameters, I figured the best offense was to keep quiet and keep him talking. "So why do *you* acknowledge sickness?"

"Because I don't believe that being sick means you should automatically die. I mean, everyone dies, but surely there is something we could do . . . *should* do about it. I mean, everyone knows that coffee will help you stay awake . . . right?"

I was not sure whether I should agree or not. So I gave him a small nod.

Ozzy's leg was jumping up and down. Boys do that when they are nervous. "If you're sleepy and you drink coffee to help you stay awake, why can't you do other things to help you feel better?"

"It sounds logical to me."

We sat in silence. He said, "I've never seen you at the archives before. Was it your first time?"

I swallowed, then nodded.

"Do you know what's in the folders?"

"Tell me," I said.

"They're testimonials, diaries, journals, writings . . . from people who looked like us, talked like us, acted like us, but were not us. They had somehow come from different worlds . . . aliens from parallel universes. These writings were left behind after they died. They'd had a totally different view—an alien view of sickness. Iona Boyd has made it her life work to study the writings of these aliens. She . . ." He shook his head. "I shouldn't say anymore." He stared at me. "Because I really don't know who you are."

I knew who I was and I knew where I had come from. The nightmare that Zeke, Joy, and I all shared seemed more and more real. Was it possible that we actually *fell* through the cave and suddenly plunged into the new but strange world? Were we like the aliens he was talking about? If so, what happened to me in my previous world? Did I suddenly disappear from that? Were my old parents looking for me? My heart was beating so fast I could barely contain it in my chest.

Should I trust him or not?

It wasn't a matter of choice. It was a matter of necessity. If I were to continue to survive in this world, I had to know the rules.

"What would you say"—I swallowed hard—"if I told you, I might . . ." I couldn't say it aloud. "If I might know one of those aliens?"

He stared at me. "I would tell you that I need to meet her and the sooner the better."

"How do you know it's a she?"

"Because I'm looking at her." He leaned over until our faces were inches apart. I could feel his breath. "Tell me about *your* world," he begged me. "Please! I have to *know*."

"You go first," I told him.

We were at a standstill, but I wasn't going to budge.

At last he nodded. "When my mom got sick, I couldn't really accept that nothing could be done . . . that all I could do was watch her die. So I did some research on my own at the local libraries and on the internet. Know what I found?"

I shook my head.

He connected his index finger to his thumb to form an O. "Nothing. A big fat zero! Okay, so you don't interfere with the natural order, but at least there must be a single piece of information that could tell me why she couldn't get out of bed, right?"

"I would think so."

"But you'd be wrong. There was nothing! No one would tell me why she couldn't see straight." He rubbed the side of his head. "Or why she had trouble in the bathroom. Or why she was so . . . tired and sad all the time."

"If you're sick all the time, you get sad, Ozzy."

"But *why* is she sick?"

How did I start explaining health to him? "It could be a lot of things. You can't ask anyone about it?"

"Too much curiosity about sickness marks you as a deviant. You can get written up, and that'll land you in jail."

My eyes grew wide.

"Crazy, huh, but it's true. But there are crazy things everywhere. A person once told me the aliens have laws where *natural* things like marijuana can land you in jail. Is that true?"

I still didn't want to divulge too much. I was the alien, not he. "Well, I've heard that some people think that marijuana can be dangerous."

"That's crazy! It's one of the few things people can use here to feel better."

"Uh, I think that in the other world that you were referring to . . . uh, I think there are better things than marijuana for things like pain. Things like aspirin or Tylenol or even stronger medicine if you need it."

"Medicine . . . oh my God, you said the word!" He got really excited. "That's the stuff that makes you feel better, right?'

"Right."

"So it really does exist."

"I think so." At the moment, I wasn't sure of anything.

"But the medicines are not natural, right?"

"Well, medicines don't grow on trees, if that's what you mean. But they're safe to use . . . if you use them correctly." My eyes met his. This wasn't the time or place to notice, but I couldn't help myself. He really was hot. "What did you do when you didn't find anything in the library or on the internet?"

"I tried to be discreet and ask a few people. No one was willing to help and I didn't want to bring too much attention to what I was doing. Still, I just couldn't sit with the fact that people get sick and then drop off the planet." He shuddered. "You know, the cleanup crew."

I wasn't looking directly at Ozzy, but I could sense his stinging eyes in my peripheral vision.

"Mom became weaker and weaker," he went on. "I didn't want what happened to Dad to happen to her. I couldn't really get my mind around the fact that she was doomed. So I started doing my own investigation."

"Hence the archives."

"No, we're not there yet."

"Sorry."

The doorbell rang. It was the pizza delivery man.

"Hold on." Ozzy got up, opened the door, and paid the guy. He took the hot box and placed it between us on the couch. Then he went to his kitchen and fetched napkins and plastic forks. "I'm real formal, as you can see."

"This is perfect." I took a wedge of pineapple and mushroom pie and ate just to show him I was okay. But I really wasn't hungry. I wanted him to finish up the story. After he polished off two slices, he attacked the pasta salad.

"Want some?"

"No, I'm fine."

"How about something to drink?"

"Water is fine."

He got up and came back with two bottles. "You never drink from the tap unless you boil it. You know that."

My mouth dropped open. I'd been drinking tap water all week. "No chlorination?"

"I don't know what that is."

"It's stuff that makes the water safe." *Where I come from*, I added in my head. "It's okay to boil water here?"

"Boiling is natural." He looked at my plate. "You hardly ate. You know what they say around here."

"What?"

"If you don't eat, that's a bad sign."

I wonder what this world would think of my world's anorexia. "No, I'm fine. Honestly. I'm just . . . intrigued with what you're telling me."

He nodded and wiped his mouth. "Yeah, I started investigating. . . ." His expression became faraway. "I began wandering around the city hoping that maybe there was something I didn't know about. I would sleep until about two, three in the morning and then get up and explore other areas of the city. Maybe there were some hidden secrets in the shadows." His eyes softened. "Please eat something, Kaida."

"I picked another piece of pineapple off the pizza. "Go on."

"I found places. Not the best places, but welcoming. I felt like I had a family again."

"What kind of places?"

"Places where you can learn about weird stuff . . . the kind of things that adults don't tell you about. The kind of weird stuff that I later read about in the archives. Medicine!" Ozzy steadied himself. "James was one of the first guys I met in the streets. After we got to talking, he sat me down on the sidewalk one night, and said, 'Okay, Oz, you're pretty smart and you seem trustworthy. I'm gonna let you in on four secrets.'"

Apparently James had a Brooklyn accent.

"'One,'" Ozzy-as-James continued, "'not everything that's allowed here is allowed somewhere else. Two, not everything allowed somewhere else is allowed here. Three, the people allowing things and stopping things here don't know shit. Four, the people going against the people in charge are the smart ones.'"

Ozzy broke into a dazzling smile.

"'Oh, there's a five,' James told me. 'We're those smart

people.'" His voice became so soft I could barely hear him. "James told me about spills, Kaida. He's a spill dealer." There was a long pause. *"I'm* a spill dealer!"

Spills, I thought. My brother had used that word. "That's illegal, right?"

"Completely illegal. Like you-can-be-arrested-and-thrown-into-jail-without-a-trial illegal. The saying goes, 'Spills kill,' but that's not true. They can kill, but if you use them right, they can help. I know they can help. They've helped my mom, especially with her pain. But they're not allowed, because they go against the Naturalist Doctrine."

"I get it." Well, I sort of got it. It appeared that Ozzy was like some sort of a "good" drug dealer. I wondered if that's how he supported his mother and himself.

"The archives in Hawthorne Library are one of the few sources of information about diseases and manufactured spills—or medicine as you call it—that cure sickness."

"Then how come everyone doesn't just go there and find the cure for the diseases they have?"

"Because one, they don't know about it, and two, you saw for yourself how hard it is to get into it. Plus even if you do get permission from a scientist like Iona Boyd and get into the archives, if you go too often, you're stigmatized."

I thought of something. "Ozzy, why can't Iona Boyd help you with your mother?"

"She's not interested in *helping* anyone, in going against the Doctrine. To her, the archives are for research, not something to use in everyday life. I read these accounts and do reports for her—that's how I work with her and how I get to use the archives."

"That's crazy," I told him. "I would think anyone who would invent medicine to cure people would be a hero."

"You would think and you'd be wrong."

Tears welled up in my eyes. I whispered, "I guess I am an alien."

He took my hand and briefly gazed at me with wonderment.

Looking at me like I was something special . . . like I was a gift from heaven.

12

Although it took me an hour to walk home from Ozzy's, time passed quickly as I thought about everything he had told me. We were all going to meet in a few hours, and I wondered how I would pull off being casual when my brain felt like it was on fire and my heart continually thumped in my chest.

Lucky for me that when the anointed time rolled around, Mom was involved with Suzanne. Lucky also that Jace wasn't home. Otherwise there would have been a barrage of questions. As it was, I ran out with an "I'll see you later." I thought Mom mumbled a good-bye, but I couldn't be sure.

The car that Ozzy wrangled up was a heap: no air-conditioning, no heat, no radio, springs sticking out of the upholstery; but it worked, so I didn't complain. He looked a lot better than the car. He said, "Driving is important to me. I need to travel across the states to these obscure places you wouldn't even believe. And since I'm still in school, I have to do it during vacation time."

His expression was serious, but his eyes were still gorgeous.

Oh, Kaida, this is so not the time to get moony. Damn those hormones. Silly schoolgirl. I started asking questions to hide my embarrassment. "Ozzy, are herbal remedies allowed? Things like mint tea for digestion?"

"Sure. Natural is good; not natural is bad. You've got to get that through your head, okay?"

"Okay. And it's fear that keeps it that way."

"Yes."

"Even if it prevents someone from saving his own life?"

"Fear of death from the authorities versus fear of death from sickness. With one you're eliminated, and with the other you get to die horribly. You choose."

"That's crazy!"

"There are always ridiculous rules. James told me that there were some people in the alien worlds that didn't use medicine for their babies to help them with sickness. Is that true?"

"No, it's not true!" I froze. "Unless you mean vaccines."

"I don't know what that is."

"Um . . . there might be some who think that vaccines—

135

which are medicines to keep you from getting sick—that they might cause autism or an allergic reaction, so yes, there are some people who don't vaccinate their babies."

"So someone convinced those people that the solution was worse than the diseases. Welcome to my world, Kaida. Welcome to my life."

Crazy, crazy, crazy. I didn't want to think about any worlds right now. But I had to. I had to focus.

"James also told me that he learned from the archives that the medicine in the alien world costs a lot of money."

"It can. But you need that stuff to take care of life."

"But you don't need it if you think that using it is dangerous."

"That's just ignorance. I think you have to turn left here to get to Joy's house."

He turned left.

"Don't look at me like I'm crazy, Kaida. I'm with you on this one. I think that survival of the fittest has its place—but not in everything." He paused. "Not when it comes to my mother."

"Turn here. She should be just over the hill." I sat up straight. "Ozzy, when you use the archives, how do they keep track of who goes and who doesn't?"

"When the library scans your archives ID, the signals are sent to the state and federal governments. James's father, Mr. Reighton, used to work for the state."

"James, the spill dealer."

"Yep. Mr. Reighton related all this information to James

right before he died." He turned to me. "We need you, Kaida. It wasn't that you recognized sickness. We all know sickness. It's that you didn't understand why no one was doing anything about it. You came here from somewhere else. And that somewhere else is where we can get help."

"But I'm here now."

"If you got in, there has to be a way to get out."

That was a childish thought. "Not everything works in reverse, Ozzy. It's like a prism. Light goes in one way and comes out another way. It's still light but vastly different."

"Or maybe not." Ozzy became sheepish. "You and your friends are the first people from the alien world that I've actually met. Before you, I'd just heard about it from James. Like Erin White . . ."

"What about her?"

"They say she moved away. But I'm wondering if she went back. That's what I heard. Am I right?"

I had no idea. I kept quiet.

He tapped the steering wheel. "You have her ID. How'd you get it?"

"It's a forgery." I felt bad about lying, but I wasn't about to implicate my brother.

"It's a good one, then."

"Look, Ozzy, this is too much for me to handle alone. I'm glad we're getting Joy and Zeke involved. I'm finding it hard to do things without them these days."

"They were with you when it happened, right?"

"We think we were all together. We're having a hard time figuring out if it was real or not."

"It was real," Ozzy said. "Believe me, it was real."

We drove up a block and then he parked. "You want to get Joy or should I?"

"I'll do it." I hesitated. "Ozzy, you said I knew the secret code. What were you talking about?"

He averted his gaze. "It's the code that spill dealers use to identify ourselves."

"What is it?"

"But you said it."

"I don't know what I said." I took his arm. "If I have to trust you, you have to trust me." I waited, then said softly, "What's the code, Ozzy?"

He let out a deep breath. "Nine-one-one."

Joy wasn't home, much to my irritation. When we arrived at Zeke's house, Anderson answered the door in his pajamas: a thing of confidence.

"Dressed for bed already?" I greeted him.

"Just being comfortable."

"Is Joy here? She's not home."

"Uh . . . I forgot to call you. . . . She walked over about an hour ago. Sorry."

"It's fine." I wanted to yell at him, to tell him we couldn't afford to waste time, but what was the use? "You met Ozzy this afternoon."

Zeke gave a quick nod, and their hands crashed in a flurry of testosterone. "Invite us inside, Zeke."

"Yeah, sure . . . sorry."

"Where's Joy now?"

"She's in my room."

We stepped inside.

There were framed photographs everywhere. And it smelled like a combination of fresh-baked cookies and Pine-Sol. There were bronzed baby shoes in the shelves and height charts tacked onto the walls, marking Zeke's and Zeke's sister's first ten years of growth.

"Who's your decorator?" I said.

"Not me, okay?" Zeke led us up the stairs and into his room. "Lay off."

"Sorry." I hadn't noticed how tense Zeke was.

His room was exceptionally neat. The bed was made, the floor was clear, and I could see the surface of his desk. There was a wall unit completely filled with trophies—from T-ball to first place in a recent swim meet. Plus there were all his debate and Model UN statues. Joy was sitting cross-legged on the floor, staring at the wall, holding her arm. She was still wearing that sweater.

Ozzy regarded the trophies. "Nice going."

Zeke gave a shrug. He clenched his jaw as he spoke. "You know, I've got a lot of pressure on me. I don't care about winning, but my parents do. Joy and I have been talking. I think I'm done with this investigation crap."

"What?" I shrieked, then covered my mouth. *"Why?"*

"Because I'm tired, Kaida, and I don't have time. I have three papers to write, a bill to defend for debate team, and a swim meet tomorrow at six in the morning. I know that things are weird. But to me, I'm home." Zeke gave out a forced laugh.

"You're willing to live in a world where the sick are left to die?"

"I don't know if that's true."

"Of course it is," I said. "Ozzy will tell you—"

Zeke held up his hand to quiet me down. "I'm here, Kaida. I'll make the best of whatever it is."

"I can't do this alone, Zeke."

"You're not alone," Ozzy said.

"I can't help you," Zeke said. "You're a different person, Kaida. I'm not like you. I'm . . . more conventional. I can't just jump headfirst into something I don't know about. I can't afford to be different anymore."

Joy whipped out a pack of cigarettes.

"Not here!" Zeke grabbed the cigarettes from Joy and threw them in the garbage. "Not now."

"Those are imported!" she nearly cried.

"It's still my house. Besides, we know what's good and what's bad."

"You do, but I don't." Ozzy intervened. "Why is smoking bad?"

We all stared at him. Finally I said to Zeke, "Do you have a few minutes? It may make a big difference in your attitude."

"My attitude is fine."

"Please," I implored him. "Just *listen* to what Ozzy has to say."

Joy said, "What would it hurt, Zeke?"

Finally he nodded. "I'll listen. Shoot."

Ozzy breathlessly launched into a summary of everything he had told me back at his house and on the car ride over.

"Wowzers," I said. It was just as amazing in recap as it was the first time.

"We have the archives," Ozzy went on. "But we need so much more. We need the knowledge that you have. Things like tobacco being bad for you. How did you get here . . . into my world?"

Joy said, "We're not certain. We've never really talked about it in depth."

"It started with our class trip to Carlsbad Caverns," Zeke said.

"Never heard of it," Ozzy said.

"They're caves in New Mexico," I told him.

"Caves . . . you came through *caves*?"

"Yeah, but not the famous caves in the national park," I said. "It was a different cave. It was hidden . . . where we had the accident."

Zeke said, "Why don't *I* start at the beginning?"

"It may be *your* beginning," I said, "but it might not be my beginning."

"Yeah, that's true. We've never compared stories. So I'll

start, and then you guys can jump in whenever you want."

He did and we did. After twenty minutes, it was remarkable how much we had remembered and how much we agreed on.

"I suppose we need to go back through the desert," Joy said.

"That shouldn't be so hard to do," Zeke said. "We crashed during our class trip. But our actual class trip in this world hasn't happened yet. So maybe we could do it then and reverse what happened. Does that make sense?"

"Not totally," I said. "What if we don't crash?"

"And who wants Mr. Addison to die?" Zeke said. "He might have something to say about that!"

"Maybe he doesn't have to die," I said.

Joy said, "Even if he doesn't wind up dying and we go through the cave again, who knows what could happen? We could end up somewhere else . . . not here, but not in our world either. There may be thousands of worlds out there that we don't know about."

That was a sobering thought. We all chewed on it for a few seconds. Then I said, "Even if we do get back, it might mean we're permanently back."

"No, that won't help . . ." Ozzy mumbled. "You need to be able to come back here."

"We can't guarantee that," I said. "Besides, I don't want to come back, Ozzy. It's terrifying in your world."

"But you need to help us."

"No, that's *not* what we need," Zeke said. "We need to either get on with our lives here or go back to where we came from."

I said, "Why don't you come with us, Ozzy?"

"Because you three were the ones who came in and out. I don't know what would happen to me."

"And we don't know what's going to happen to us," Joy said. "If we're going to take a chance, you should go, too."

"But my mom needs me."

I said, "Then why did you even bother asking me—asking us—for help?"

Ozzy said, "Because if you guys can go in and out, you could help us identify an infinite number of diseases! We'd know symptoms and possibly cures. You could bring back actual made-for-disease medicine!"

"And get arrested?" I pointed out. "Besides, we're not doctors. We could mix up diseases just as easily as you could. Once when I thought I had a cold, the doctor told me it was pneumonia."

Ozzy said, "Doctors are like legal professional spill dealers, right?"

"No, legal spill dealers would be like drug manufacturers," I told him.

Joy screamed from out of nowhere.

"What is it?" Zeke commanded, his eyes growing huge.

"Pain in my arm!" She was trembling.

"She hurt her arm when she fell through the cave," I said. "Let me look at it."

When she peeled off her sweater, I gasped. The arm was red and swollen.

"It looks infected, Joy," Zeke told her. "You need to go to the doct—"

Awkward amplified. I looked at Zeke's bed. The neatness reminded me of the doctor's office that we couldn't go to.

Zeke said, "We need to treat you somehow, Joy. Because if we don't . . ."

Ozzy finished the thought. "That could be very bad."

13

"So what the hell do I do?" Joy yelped.

I knelt beside her. "I don't know, but we're going to do something."

"Like *what*?"

My brain was going a mile a minute. "Okay . . . okay . . . hey! What about chemistry?" I looked at Ozzy. "I know that there's chemistry here. I've taken it in school. Maybe we can *make* drugs."

He let out a small laugh. "What do you think I've been talking about, Kaida?"

"Oh . . . okay." I patted his arm. "So I guess that means

you're the go-to guy right now."

Zeke said, "Kaida's got a point, Ozzy. You may be making or dealing the stuff, but *we* know what stuff works."

"He's right!" Joy was still clutching her arm. "Zeke could help a lot. He's good at chem."

"Zeke, we'll take all the help we can get," Ozzy told him. "And we'd love for you to get involved. But I've got to be fair to you. You gotta know what you're getting yourself into. It's not just against the law, it's jail time . . . and sometimes even worse."

Joy said, "Worse, meaning . . ."

No one spoke.

"You know, I just thought about something," I said. "When we took seventh grade science in our former life, didn't we read about moldy cheese containing penicillin?"

Zeke sat up. "I've got Roquefort cheese in the kitchen. That's moldy. Hold on."

Ozzy looked at me. "I think I've read about pencellus . . ."

"Penicillin . . . it helps fight infection," I told him. "Where did you read about it?"

"In one of the papers from the archives." He looked confused. "What about moldy cheese?"

"I'll explain later. I want to read those papers that you took out. I need to know what's so valuable that it almost got Zeke and Joy arrested at the archives."

"It's okay with me, but it's getting late," Ozzy said. "Your parents may say something. Last thing I want is to drag you down with me."

"Ozzy, I don't do anything I don't want to do." I was pacing a very small space when Zeke came up a moment later. "Stuff yourself with this."

Joy began cramming her mouth full of very expensive cheese. Within seconds the room smelled like a French café. Between bites, she said, "Zeke really is a chemistry genius."

"She's exaggerating." He was acting offhanded, but I could tell he was feeling good about the compliment. There was more than school chemistry going on between the two of them. To Ozzy, Zeke said, "I hope you have something better than Roquefort for her arm."

"So now you're down with the program?" Ozzy asked.

"Joy's arm changes the whole thing," he said. "We have to help her."

Ozzy grinned. "Great. So I'll go to James tomorrow night and we'll figure it out. We'll get you fixed up as best we can. But it may take a few days. Like I said, it's dangerous."

I said, "Once we get rid of Joy's infected arm, then we'll move on to other things."

"Like what?" Ozzy asked.

"Like getting the hell out of here and getting back to where we came from," Zeke said.

The room fell silent. Zeke had articulated my thoughts exactly, and judging by the expression on Joy's face, it appeared she had been thinking the same thing.

Ozzy, on the other hand, agreed with Zeke for an entirely different reason. "Yeah, if you could get back to your world and then, if you could somehow make it back here, imagine how much good you could do! It would be . . . you have no idea how many sick people are running from the authorities!"

Zeke looked down as if to say, "You don't get it." Out loud he said, "One problem at a time."

"Agreed," Joy said, still wolfing down cheese. "Ugh, this is really strong! I sure hope I'm not eating all this fat for nothing!"

Zeke faked a yawn. "I'm beat, guys, and I have a swim meet. So as much as I hate to be rude . . ."

"I understand," I told him. "Look, it's important that we act as normal as possible under the rules here, right?"

"Don't have to tell me twice," Joy said. "I'm not showing my arm to anyone!"

"Good." I turned to Ozzy. "I still want to read those papers."

"Then let's go."

We gave one another hugs good-bye. I routinely did that with my friends, so I guess that meant that Joy and Zeke were now my friends. But it was more than that. It was the kind of hug that I bet people gave each other on the Titanic: Maybe I'll see you again, but maybe I won't.

* * *

I sat on Ozzy's couch staring at the pizza box from this afternoon.

"I have leftovers. You want me to warm them up?"

"I'm not too hungry and I don't have a lot of time," I told him. "But thanks."

"I'll get the papers."

I had yet to meet Ozzy's mother. She was sleeping when I arrived this afternoon and she was sleeping now. It was around nine-thirty in the evening and I had about an hour before I'd start receiving phone calls from my mother.

Where are you!

I didn't want to call in—my voice sounded shaky to my ears. So that would mean I had to be home in about forty-five minutes. I had about a half hour at Ozzy's house.

He came back holding an envelope close to his chest. "This is a protective covering for the material."

"Okay . . . what am I looking at?"

"Statements by people who claim they came from somewhere else."

"People like me?"

"I suppose so, although I don't really know where you came from, so it could be a world that's different from yours."

"Do they write about medicine?"

"They write about themselves." Ozzy's face was very intense. "Once I take the papers out, you've got to keep them in the glassine folder and you've got to be quick. You heard Luckman. Not more than two minutes each, so that really means about a minute and a half. If they fade, I'm in deep shit!"

"I'm ready."

He took the first folder out of the envelope and looked at his watch. "Go."

The first one dealt with a woman named Sarah. She claimed she drowned and woke up in her own bed. She thought she had a bad dream. She didn't notice anything until she went to work the next day. She was a nurse before, but the doctor's office was gone. Furthermore no one knew what a nurse was—"

"Time."

I gave the material back to him. "I just started."

"I know. That's what's so frustrating."

"How do you read so fast?"

"Kaida, you learn to cope with all sorts of things when you operate outside the boundaries. You ready for number two?"

"Yep."

"Here you go." His eyes were on his wrist. "Go!"

A doctor who committed suicide. He woke up in bed at home and couldn't figure out why he was still alive. But he was happy he was. He ate breakfast, then decided he really needed psychological and physical help. He drove himself to the hospital where he worked, but it wasn't there. No one knew what he was talking about. No one knew what a doctor was. His wife told him that he was an engineer—"

"Time."

"Damn!"

"I know, it goes really fast."

"I wish I was a speed reader."

"If you keep doing this long enough, you will be. Number three coming up."

"Lay it on me."

This guy was a drug salesperson. He worked for Mercy Pharmaceuticals. He had a traffic accident and when he woke up, he was in his own bed. He thought it was a bad dream. He got up to go to work, but instead of finding Mercy, he found a company named Harding that made industrial paints. He couldn't figure out what happened to his company. He finally found a coworker and asked him about it, but the coworker had no idea what he was talking about—"

"Time."

"Arg!" I handed him back the folder. "This is exasperating!"

"Tell me about it," Ozzy said. "So now you know the crap I'm dealing with. Also, once I return these folders tomorrow, I can't go back to the archives for another four months without arousing suspicion. Iona Boyd has a ton of assistants. They like it that way. It means no one person knows too much."

"Who's *they*?" I asked.

"They . . . she . . . I don't know *everything*." He frowned and I could tell he was bothered. "I *do* know that you can't visit the archives too often without someone asking probing questions. I know because it's happened to me."

"Wow. Sorry if I screwed something up for you."

"No, no." He put the protective envelope down and took my hand. "You're one of the gifted. You know stuff! Like about moldy cheese. Tell me about moldy cheese."

I noticed he was still holding my hand. When he realized I was looking down at our interlaced fingers, he blushed and gently pulled his hand from mine.

"Some moldy food has natural penicillin in it."

"And what is penicillin again?"

"It's called an antibiotic. It helps kill the stuff that makes you sick."

"What kind of stuff?"

"Bacteria . . . which are like little invisible bugs." His expression was even more perplexed. It sounded crazy to my ears. I could surmise what it sounded like to him. "You'll have to take my word for it."

"I do, I do."

"Anyway, things like moldy cheese . . . sharp cheese like Roquefort." I bit my lower lip. "I think also moldy, unprocessed salami . . . they help fight the germs." I looked into his eyes. "This was something I picked up from my seventh-grade science class. I was twelve or thirteen and way more interested in boys and music than I was in science." I didn't tell him that I was still that way . . . or had been until the accident.

"You must be on to something," Ozzy said. "Zeke and Joy understood right away. So if I took cheese and let it rot and fed it to my mom, it would help her?"

"I don't know, Ozzy. I don't know what's making your mom sick."

Again he nodded, but he seemed dejected. "What did you think of the material?"

"They all had a couple of things in common," I said. "Something terrible happened. The people woke up the next morning in their beds thinking they'd had bad dreams. And then they discovered that their world—that included medicine and health care—had just . . . disappeared."

"How similar is that to your story?"

"Identical, actually." I paused. "Ozzy, have you read anything where a person consistently went back and forth between the two worlds?"

"No. But that doesn't mean it can't happen." He took my hand again. "Maybe you can be the first one!"

"I'm fifteen years old."

"Joan of Arc was fifteen when she led the troops and defeated the English."

At least we were learning the same history. "She was burned at the stake." I pulled my hand away. "I need to get home, Ozzy."

"Absolutely." He stood up and so did I. "I know I'm putting a lot of pressure on you, Kaida. I just want to tell you how grateful I am . . . grateful that I met you."

"It's good for both of us. We need help with Joy's arm."

"I'll get on it right away."

"I'm sorry that I'm not Joan of Arc."

"Don't be sorry, Kaida. I understand what you're saying."

Of course he understood, but still I could tell that he was disappointed.

14

When I got home, Jace was planted on the couch, crumbs all over his face, his eyes on the television screen.

"How's it going?" I asked my brother.

"Keep it down. Suzanne's asleep."

I love you, too, I thought. "Isn't this supposed to be your toughest year of high school?"

"That's eleventh grade. Twelfth is much easier." He was still involved in the tube. "Besides, it's the weekend, and since you stuck me with babysitting, I figured I'd make the best of it." He finally looked up. "Where were you?"

"Just around." I made my escape into the kitchen. A bowl of cookie dough sat on the counter. I accidentally knocked over a spoon. It clanged on the floor, and upstairs my sister began to wail.

"Freakin'-A, Kaida! One night, I figure I can get her to sleep and just chill until Mom and Dad get home. But no!"

"I'll get her." I ran upstairs to Suzanne's room, which was painted lavender because my mom read somewhere it promoted "zen."

Suzanne was shrieking.

Calm shmalm.

I picked her up, rocking her while singing her to sleep. It took some time, but I wasn't in a hurry. I didn't want to deal with my brother. When she'd finally quieted, I tucked her in the crib and went downstairs. Jace was still in front of the television. I went back to the kitchen and took out some left-over pasta. Jace came in a minute later. His black shorts were covered with food stuff.

"Sorry if I'm a little tense."

"No biggie. Want some pasta?"

"No, I'm okay." He didn't look okay. "I heard you visited the archives."

"Yeah . . . I was only there for about five minutes and I didn't even go inside." I gave him the best smile I could manage. "Where did you hear that?"

"Some people saw you at Hawthorne. I guess I just figured

you took my advice—which I might not have been so bright to give you."

I tried to act casual. "You can have the ID back. I don't think I'll be going there again."

"Phew!" he said. "That's good."

"Who is Erin White?"

"She's no one. Don't mention her, okay?"

"Trouble?"

"It's not important. Where's her ID?"

"In my purse."

Immediately he got up and rooted through my mess until he found the beaten-up ID. He stared wistfully at the picture. "So it got you into the archives or . . ."

"Yeah, it worked, but I only spent a few minutes down there. Have you ever been?"

"No."

"I don't know why you sent me there. It's very confusing."

"Yeah, I must have had brain freeze. I'm glad everything worked out okay."

I nodded. "You're right. It's stupid to ask so many unanswerable questions."

"Good for you!" Jace smiled. "You're a much quicker learner than I am."

"How about if I take the pasta into the living room and we share it?"

"Sounds good."

I followed him into the living room a few minutes later with two bowls of penne pasta.

Jace said, "One more thing. People are also saying that you've been hanging around that kid, Ozzy Callahan."

I froze.

"You are?" Jace looked ill.

I didn't answer him. There was only so much lying I could do in a day.

"Look, he's bad news, Kaida." He put his hand on my shoulder. "Not the way Maria is bad news—Ozzy is actually *bad news.* Don't hang out with him."

Sometimes we lived in too small a town. We ate for a few moments in silence. Then I said, "I just talked to him a couple of times."

"That's not what I heard."

"Maybe you got the wrong information." I gave him the rest of the pasta. "How about if I bake cookies and we eat them all before Mom and Dad get home."

"Kaida, I mean it. He hangs around the wrong—"

"I don't particularly need your advice at this time, thanks."

"This isn't advice. Advice implies you can take it or leave it. This is a warning from your brother who cares deeply about you."

His concern was reason enough to worry. Jace is not the sentimental type.

"Your advice is duly registered." I kissed the top of his head. "I have to call Maria. I'll see you later."

"You promise it's Maria you're calling?"

"God!" I scolded him. "Enough of the big brother crap, okay? I heard what you said, I'll take it into consideration, and yes, I'm calling Maria."

I made certain that when I got to my room, I closed the door softly. I didn't want to have to deal with Jace or Suzanne.

"Hey shugapie," I said when she picked up the line.

"Hi," Maria croaked on the other end of the telephone.

"Whoa, are you—" Sick, I wanted to say. But I caught myself. "How are you doing?"

"I'm great," she proclaimed.

"Great."

She burst into tears.

"Oh, God, Kaida," Maria said. "I really hope it's temporary. But what if it's not? What if it stays? I'm scared. I'm so freaking scared!" She sobbed, her breaths coming out scratchy through the receiver.

"Of course it'll go away," I said with authority. I wanted to say it's only a cold, but I had to put myself in her position. This is what I'd have to worry about every day if I remained here. Oh, how I wanted to go back. How I wanted to take everyone I loved with me. "You know it'll go away and so do I."

"Kaida, how can you honestly say that?" she said between hacks.

"Cause I know these things. You've had this before and it went away, right?"

"Right."

"So this one will, too."

"Oh, Kaida, you really know how to say the right things." And with that she sneezed.

"You know, one day . . . maybe they'll fix this."

"Fix what?"

"You know . . . getting sick."

"Everyone gets sick."

"Okay, yeah, you're right. But some people . . . they don't stay sick even if they're very sick." She didn't answer. "Hello?"

"I hear you. Don't talk smack, Kaida."

"It's not smack." I bit my bottom lip and tugged on one pigtail, "Like you know . . . there are ways to help when you're sick."

"I'm drinking hot tea."

"I mean something more—"

"Don't go there."

"Go where?"

"Spills," she whispered.

"I know one. A spill dealer. If you need help—"

"Do you have . . ." She sneezed. "Do you have any conception at all of how ridiculously insane that is?"

"Maria"—my voice was tender—"you wore different-colored socks in kindergarten. You convinced me to dye my hair purple." I hesitated, because Jace could've been listening, "You made me do a shot of vodka! I think you know insane pretty well." Even if alcohol wasn't illegal in this parallel universe, it was a pariah for me in my brother's universe.

"Kaida, this is beyond ugly clothing." Her voice was trembling. "This will screw up our lives if we get caught."

"Getting caught is for the stupid teenagers." I smiled slyly, even if she couldn't see it. "And since when have we been anything like them?"

Dear God, I thought, *whatever you are, at least return my Maria to me.*

Then she said, "You've got a point there, Hutchenson. But before we take a serious step . . . let's see what happens with me."

"That sounds reasonable."

"Kaida, thank you, thank you, for being the kind of friend who would do that for me. I hope that I would be the kind of friend who would do that for you."

"Of course you would."

She sneezed. "I'd better get back to my tea. It's the only thing that makes me feel good. Talk to you later."

"Bye." I hung up and felt pretty positive about the conversation. Then I remembered that she didn't ask who the spill dealer was and how I knew him.

It set me to thinking.

Jace knew I had been hanging around Ozzy. How did *he* find out?

No, Maria would never do that. She'd never talk behind

my back—especially to my brother.

Unless . . .

Unless she thought it was for my own good.

I was awakened by a pounding on my door. I heard my mother's voice, but I could barely understand her.

". . . up right now!" I heard my mother yell. Aroused from a deep sleep, I thought I heard two men arguing. Suzanne was wailing in the background.

"Just rock her to sleep, Mom," I told her.

"Don't you dare talk back to me," my mom snapped, opening my door and turning on my light.

"Mom, what—"

"If you're not downstairs in two minutes, you can expect something a lot worse than lack of sleep in your future." My mother looked like she was about to pop a blood vessel. Her face was red, but her eyes appeared as if she had been crying.

"Fine!" I got up. "I'll put her back to sleep!"

But when I reached for the baby, she turned her away protectively. "Kaida, this doesn't concern putting your sister back to sleep! Come downstairs now!"

I rubbed my eyes, but I still wasn't quite awake. I was dreaming about the time my mother had fainted while coming out of the bath. Dad had picked her up and Jace had called the ambulance. If that had happened now, there'd be no ambulance to call.

"It could mean nothing!" I heard my brother shout. At

least I think I heard him. It was very hard for me to distinguish between dreams and reality.

"Jace, shut up!" my father snapped back. "You're a kid and you don't know anything about anything!"

Since when was the Hutchenson residence a made-for-Lifetime-TV special?

My father saw me coming down the stairs and stopped yelling at Jace. "Sit," he commanded. "You too," he said to my brother.

So there we were, parked in our living room, my parents on the couch and Jace and I in the wingback chairs opposite them, the only sound my little sister's wailing.

"Oh, for God's sake, can someone take care of Suzy?" My mother rubbed her temples.

"Sure." I started to rise, but my father held up his hand. "Jace, go."

He got up without a word, took the baby, and went upstairs.

My father attempted a smile. "All right, Kaida, I'm going to try and make my point as succinctly as possible. You've always been a bit of a cheeky girl. A little spunky, keeping us on edge. But you've never given us *trouble*. Trouble, Kaida, is something you've managed to avoid until now."

"I'm not in trouble." I thought I sounded very brave and confident.

"Don't interrupt your father," Mom said sternly.

"May I continue?" My father tapped his index finger

against his cheek. I didn't dare answer the rhetorical question. That should have alerted him that something was wrong with me. But he was too caught up in what was happening.

He started again. "People have been talking."

"Saying what?"

"Among other things, that you're hanging out with the wrong sort of people. Tell me, Kaida, do you find endangering your family cool?"

"I'm not endangering anyone," I croaked out.

"Do the words *spill dealer* have any meaning to you?"

Damn it, Jace. It was the last time I was going to trust him—ever.

"Jace was bad enough. He's a boy and boys do stupid things. But you? Are you trying to get us all arrested?"

I blanched. "No! Of course—"

"I don't care if this is some ridiculous teenage rebellion. I have no patience for it anymore. If I hear anything more about it, then you're out of this house!" my father roared.

I sat there and blinked, too stunned to cry. My mother took care of that for me. She burst into tears, and the look of flaming hell on my father's face melted in seconds.

"Come here, Kaida," my mother choked.

I got up from my chair and sat between them. My mother held my face in her moist palms and kissed my cheeks. "I will kill that boy before I let you hang around him." She sobbed, hugging my head.

"We love you, dragon-girl," my father told me. "That's

why we're doing this. You know that, right?"

"Of course." I smiled a little. "You're right and I'm very sorry."

"Please say that like you mean it," Dad told me.

"I do mean it." I kissed his cheek. "I'm sorry. I didn't know until Jace told me this afternoon that it was bad. Don't worry about me. Please."

"By the way, Jace wasn't the one we heard it from," Mom said.

"He defended you," my father said. "He kept saying that I shouldn't believe everything I hear." Dad shook his head. "What is it with you two? A sibling conspiracy against the parents?"

My eyes were wet with tears. "We stick up for each other. It's what you taught us." I gave them a closed-mouth smile. "Can I go to bed now?"

"Have I made myself clear?"

"Yes."

"Go to bed."

I bolted from the living room, passing Jace as he exited Suzanne's nursery.

"It wasn't me, I swear," Jace whispered. "I would never rat you out."

"I believe you, Jace." Although I wasn't sure that I did. "Good night."

I scurried back to bed, staring up at the ceiling, my eyes adjusting to the dimness. My hands were laced like I was praying, and my whole body felt like I was lying on a bed of needles. I knew I should have been frightened into submission because their concerns were real. But instead I felt calm wash over me, knowing the most successful renegades are the silent ones.

15

"Hey," Iggy said.

"Hey," I answered back. I took a seat next to him in computer lab. School was just about to let out—our English class was dismissed with five minutes to spare—and I was glad that I had gotten there early enough to find a seat. The lab was a good place to do homework.

Like homework was important. My entire perspective had changed.

"Maria was holed up for the weekend. She didn't return my calls." He scratched his frizzy orange hair. My thought was *Go take a shower.*

But what I said was "Maybe she's visiting her cousin."

"Whatever, Kaida," Iggy interrupted. "I know she's not visiting her cousin, okay? Besides, it's Tuesday and she would have been back by yesterday."

I looked at Iggy's baggy shorts and single earring and thought, *I should really punch you right now.* Having been in this life for a week or so, I had to give him the benefit of the doubt. Maybe he was speaking from concern.

"I'm sure she's fine," I responded quickly.

"Well, someone's dressed up this afternoon." I felt two hands on my shoulders and knew who it was before I turned around.

"Praise the skies!" I grabbed Maria and sprinted across the room, giving her an impromptu piggyback ride.

"I appreciate the enthusiasm," she said when I put her down. "It *was* temporary, after all."

"Told you." I was relieved that I wouldn't have to smuggle drugs—yet.

"What are you doing here after school's over?"

"I came here to get my makeup work."

"It's Buchanan. You didn't miss much. Wanna hang out?"

"I've got to go back home." She touched her throat. "Just want to be a hundred percent certain."

"I get it."

"Maria!" Iggy crushed her in a bear hug.

"Good-to-see-you-too-Ig," Maria choked out in Iggy's suffocating grasp.

Iggy let go of her. Something else caught his attention.

"Hey, K, I think your newest conquest is calling you."

I turned around. Ozzy was tapping lightly on a window leading out to the hallway. He was so tall that he had to bend down to make his head visible in the window. He gave me a half smile and gestured for me to come outside.

"Better go before people start yakking." Maria nudged me in the ribs—hard.

"Keep this to yourself . . . please?"

She made a zip across her lips. I darted out of class and found him by my locker. "How did we suddenly become a couple?"

"I don't know, but it's okay with me." His smile was dazzling.

"Me too, except there's a problem." I met his eyes. "My parents have forbidden me to see you. I mean I can see you, but I can't hang—"

"I get it." His green eyes darkened and he seemed to shrink. "I figured it was only a matter of time."

"It doesn't mean I'm going to listen . . ." I sighed. "It does mean that we need to be a little bit more careful." My eyes swept over the place. The hallways were becoming more and more crowded as students started filing out. I opened my locker. "I don't want my brother to see us talking."

He looked at the ceiling. "You shouldn't put yourself at risk for me."

"It's not for you, Ozzy—it's for Joy." When he didn't answer me, I whispered, "But I would have taken the risk for you, too."

His face became the color of a tomato. "I have news, Kaida." His eyes darted from me to the crowds. "Wait outside. I'll pick you up."

He walked away. I gave it a minute or two and then went outside and loitered around the student lot. In the meantime, I called my parents and told them I was going home with Maria and I was eating dinner there.

Mom had no trouble believing that.

Then I called Maria and asked her to cover for me. She loved the idea of playing secret agent.

I hated being duplicitous and disobeying my parents, but things needed to happen. Joy was in trouble with her arm. It was only a matter of time before the infection became obvious and started wreaking havoc on her body. If there was a time for action, it would be now. I thought about it in bed last night, rationalizing that I wasn't defying my *real* parents. They were somewhere in some other universe—at least I hoped that was the case. They couldn't possibly have traveled with me unless the entire journey was in my head. But that would mean it was in Zeke's and Joy's heads as well. And why did we know stuff that no one else knew?

It was mind-boggling to think about it—me here and me there. Did I exist simultaneously? How was that possible?

Concentrate, Kaida. Now's not the time for speculation. The point was I loathed the idea that I'd get my parents and family—whoever they really were—into trouble.

Ozzy pulled up in an ancient pickup truck with a motor

170

that sounded like a thousand vengeful cats. I hopped in. "What's the age limit for driving here? If you can smoke as soon as you can breathe, can you drive as soon as you can steer?"

"Age limit is sixteen, but most parents forbid their kids to get behind the wheel until they're eighteen. The road is a death trap."

"But you drive," I pointed out.

"Don't really have a choice. When you need to pick up and deliver stuff all the time, you need to drive." He looked over his shoulder and pulled the car out of the lot.

"So you make money, right?"

"Money?"

"Picking up and delivering spills."

"Cost only plus gas and free spills for my mom," he told me. "Least they could do when I put myself at risk."

"How do you support yourself?"

"We have a little in savings . . . not much. That's why we live like we do."

I felt bad about bringing it up, but I was glad he wasn't making a huge profit with his dealing. I decided silence was golden and turned quiet.

Ozzy said, "Sports are the big one."

"Pardon?"

"If you really want to prove your machismo, you play sports . . . knowing what could happen."

"Why would people take a risk?"

"For the glory . . . and if you're pro, it's for the money."

"But what if something happens?"

"That's the thrill, Kaida. To cheat death."

I didn't answer. I suppose it wasn't very different from racing autos, knowing that at any minute someone could lose control and crack into a wall. Still, things like basketball and baseball weren't supposed to be dangerous sports. No wonder Zeke swam instead of playing football. Not too much can happen there.

"So what's the big news?" I persisted.

"First things first. We've found some spills for Joy."

"That's great news!" I couldn't help it. I leaned over and kissed his cheek. "You're a miracle worker." I thought a moment. "You said 'first things first.' What's second on the list?"

"Second is . . . we're going to get the hell out of this world."

I wasn't sure if I heard him correctly. "*We're* going to get the hell out?"

"I need to go back with you guys so I can return and help everyone. It's just unfair to lay all of this on your shoulders."

That part was true.

"I mean, if there was a way in, there must be a way out."

"That's faulty logic." I rolled down my window for fresh air. "Things don't happen in reverse. Does the snake spit the mouse back out?" That was an expression my dad used a lot, even when it made no sense. I think he made it up.

172

"Perhaps not the mouse in its entirety, perhaps just the skeleton of the mouse." His face was a mask of focus. "I have to believe that it can be done. I have to believe that there's a better way."

I touched his shoulder as he stopped at a red light. "Don't get me wrong, I want to get out of here, too. I'm just thinking . . . what are the chances that we'll find the exact same cave we fell through? It wasn't near any significant landmark. We'd have to search miles of desert. And even if we could inspect every square foot of New Mexico, who says the cave even exists?"

"Kaida?" He kept his eyes focused on the road ahead. "How similar is your world to this world?"

"Pretty much the same in every aspect except health."

"So what would you classify this world as?" He drove as the light flashed green.

"I've thought about it and thought about it. It's like a parallel universe, but not exactly. I mean, you're here in this world, but I don't know if you were back in my original world."

"Would you say that these two worlds exist separately but simultaneously? Untouched by each other but in almost perfect similarity?"

"The key is almost, I think. And health is a pretty big factor, Oz."

He grinned. "Oz?"

"You are the wizard."

"I like it, especially coming from you." I felt my face turn hot, but he had other things in mind than flirting. "So let's say the two worlds do exist at the same time. Who was your best friend in the other world?"

"Well, Maria, of course."

"And your family, still the same?"

"Basically . . . yes."

"And your school, your classes, everything that matters to you exists here in this world."

"The same people exist, yes."

"So if everything exists in harmony with your other universe, then your class trip to Carlsbad should play out exactly as the trip that took you here . . . in this parallel universe."

"But it's not exactly the same, Ozzy—that's the point. I don't know if we can return where I came from. And I certainly don't know if anyone can go back and forth." I turned to him. "Do you know anyone who's gone back and forth?"

He shook his head no. He looked so dejected that I had to give him—and me—some hope. "It may be possible, but we don't know."

He turned down a dirty street that smelled like turnips. "Tell me what happened . . . as much as you can remember."

"You've heard the story."

"A recap, then, in your own words."

"Mr. Addison lost control of the car. We crashed and the van erupted into flames. It started to pour so we took shelter in a cave. Joy fell down a pit and we tried to rescue her. That's when we got lost." I looked at the bleak buildings we were passing. Most of them were in a state of decay. "We were in a cave for around a day, but we finally found a way out. The last thing I remember was a blinding light. Then I woke up in my bed and it was Monday morning and I had to get ready for school."

"Just like the people in the archives."

"Exactly."

Ozzy thought a moment. "Did Mr. Addison survive?"

I shook my head. "I don't think so."

"Are you sure?"

"He didn't emerge from the crash, but it was dark. I suppose it's remotely possible that he escaped and we didn't see him."

He tapped the steering wheel with his right hand. "When you go on the upcoming trip, you have to re-create that day. Then we can find the cave."

"Ozzy, how can we re-create an accident? And the exact same accident, at that? What makes you think that Mr. Addison is going to want to die?"

"Like you said, maybe he didn't die." He thought for a moment. "It's like the prism parallel you mentioned. Light goes in and light comes out."

"But the light changes from white to multicolored. It's different."

"It's different, but it's the same. The light doesn't suddenly turn into an armchair. Your world is reflected through some weird dimension, and it's coming out into this world. It's the same world, I think, just cast in a different light. Everything revolves around your class trip to Carlsbad."

"I'm going on the trip, okay?" Just thinking about it made me feel light-headed. The thought of having to re-create that nightmarish horror. "I'll go on the trip, Ozzy, but I'm not going to punch Mr. Addison so we swerve and crash. But if it's destined that we crash again, in the same way . . . then the three of us will . . . well, we'll at least know what to do. Sort of."

"I'm just figuring out how I'm supposed to go with you because I'm not a sophomore and it's not my class trip." He pulled up to a curb and parked . . . badly, I saw when we got out.

"We'll find a way to sneak you in there," I told him.

"I hope so. If I could go back and forth, I could do so much good."

I patted his hand and he smiled. In front of us was a dingy brown building with big block letters spelling out Rix Plac. I assumed the *e* had fallen off. Graffiti painted the walls. "Where are we?"

"My second home." He took my hand. "Let's go."

He opened the door, and a musty whiff assaulted my nostrils. It was crowded, and it smelled like beer and hormones. Mostly men between puberty and old age, but there were a few women. I can't say that the masses looked reputable, but they didn't look like bums, either. The dress was casual. The place had sawdust on the floors and mirrors on the walls and looked completely unoriginal, just like a thousand other shady bars I'd seen before.

On television, that is.

"Ozzy!"

"Ozster!"

"My main man, get this gentleman a drink!"

"Hey, Ozzy," an older woman on a barstool purred.

"Hey, Colbert." He dropped my hand and patted a guy in a collared shirt on the back. "Lester, long time, no see!"

"Whose fault is that?" a skinny man with a blond comb-over said.

"Hey, handsome." A striking woman with red lips, wavy black hair, and a husky voice stood up and pulled Ozzy into a big hug. "How goes it?"

"Michelle!" he hugged her back. "You look—"

"I know," she interrupted and stepped back. "I look fabulous."

I coughed. Ozzy smiled and pulled me in front of him. "Kaida, meet Michelle, James's older sister and my adopted sister."

James, as in the spill dealer. It was business. Jealousy quelled, I extended my hand. Michelle took it and smiled warmly. I wanted to ask Oz what we were doing here but knew well enough when to keep my mouth shut. There was a time for action and there was a time to take a backseat. This was caboose time.

"How's your mom?" Michelle asked Ozzy with concern.

"She's getting along." He turned to me. "I want to introduce Kaida to the famous James."

"The *infamous* James is taking a nap." Michelle pushed a curtain of hair behind her shoulder, and I felt a twinge of envy. "He was out all night, thanks to you."

"He got it?" Ozzy exclaimed.

Michelle put her finger to her lips.

"Sorry," he whispered.

"Though I dread it, I'll need to wake him up so you can get on with what you need."

"Tell you what, Meesh, I'll do the honors."

"Fair enough. He's upstairs." Michelle hugged Ozzy again. "You take care of yourself, darling. Don't make yourself so scarce. Drop in when you *don't* need something, okay?"

"Got it." He took my hand and led me to a staircase. It was dizzying and kept winding and winding and winding, as if it were saying: *Now you will throw up!* When we finally reached the top, I felt my head spin.

"You okay?"

"I dunno. I'm slightly dizzy."

"The place is a little ripe. Sorry about that." He knocked on a door with chips of green paint falling off.

We heard groaning coming from the other side of the door. "What the hell?"

"Open up, James."

"Leave me alone."

Ozzy pounded harder on the door. "Come on, man. I know you were out all night, but we've got a nine-one-one here."

Something rumbled in the room, and the door opened.

"Ozzy Callahan in the flesh."

The man who spoke was garbed in cargo pants and an oversize T-shirt. He had light brown hair that was short and spiked, and bloodshot blue eyes.

"Alive and warm-blooded." Ozzy gave James that sort of guy-hug where you slam your body against the other person and slap his back.

James rubbed his eyes and nodded toward me. "Who's this lovely lass with the purple hair?"

"As if you didn't know."

James leaned against the door frame. "Are you *the* Kaida that I've been hearing *a lot* about?"

I was rendered speechless with not a witticism to spare.

Ozzy laughed. "You're embarrassing her."

"What about you?" I asked Ozzy.

"I'm beyond embarrassment."

James laughed. "Well, as long as you're here you might as well come in."

The space was tiny, with a lumpy mattress covered with messy sheets atop a metal frame. By the edge of the cot was a scarred table, and on it were two items: a plain white lamp and a white paper bag with the ends rolled up tight.

James picked up the bag. "Sorry, man, but this'll cost you." He quoted an exorbitant price. "I'm not getting rich on this, but I gotta get some gas money."

Ozzy's complexion turned sickly green. "James, I don't have that much money. You know that."

"Sorry, but it's getting harder and harder."

"I have money." The two boys looked at me as I pulled out a stack of bills. "I raided my piggy bank."

The two of them kept staring at me.

"What? You don't believe it's real?"

"Where'd you get all that cash?" Ozzy asked me.

"Birthdays, Christmas, special occasions. When you shop secondhand and your big splurge is hair dye, you save up." I gave James the required amount. "I went to the ATM after school yesterday. This is costing me about half of what I own, so the stuff better work."

"I promise you if it doesn't, I'll make good," James assured me.

I nodded. "Okay."

James licked his lips. "Ozzy's been telling me a lot about you."

"You already said that." I was surprised by the toughness in my voice. My eyes bounced between Ozzy's eyes and James's face. "He's been telling me a lot about you."

"I hope it's all good."

I nodded.

James said, "You remind me of a girl I once knew. Tough,

smart, beautiful . . . very caring and very daring and very . . . different like you."

Erin White? Or someone like her probably. "What happened to her?"

"I hope she's in a better . . . universe." He gave a small smile. "Maybe you'll go there sometime."

"That would be nice." I crooked a thumb in Ozzy's direction. "Maybe I'll take him with me."

"Just as long as he comes back."

"That's a promise." Ozzy gave him another hug. "So I might not see you for a long time."

James smiled sadly. "Well, then . . ." He pulled something from under his mattress. It was a tiny bottle of a clear liquid. "Here."

Ozzy laughed. "That's not enough to get me drunk."

"It's not supposed to. It's for your mother . . . a good-bye gesture."

"How much?"

"On the house."

"Thanks, man. I'm running low. Thanks a lot."

James dropped the bottle into the bag and stared at me hard. "Take care of him. He isn't as smart as he thinks he is."

He tossed me the paper bag.

"There are two things in there. One for the pain and one to help with the condition."

I peered inside. There was a bottle of red tablets that looked a lot like Advil. There was also a box with chewable squares inside. They looked like chocolate if you didn't know any better. But I had had some embarrassing intestinal problems in my former life.

"Where'd you get these?" I asked.

"Someone brought them from another place," James said.

Another place . . . meaning my old world?

Assuming that people could be transported, I supposed things could be transported as well. If I could bring Coyote Cream with me from my world, maybe someone else could have brought Advil. I would have liked to question him further, but I knew we were short on time.

I said, "These look like something that might help the pain," I told him. "But these . . ." I held up the box. "I'm not a professional, but I don't think this is going to help. I think these are laxatives."

"And?" James said.

"Do you know what laxatives do?"

"The guy who sold them to me said he got it from another place and it would help her arm."

There were unscrupulous dealers in my world; why wouldn't there be unscrupulous dealers in this one as well? "In my world, laxatives help you go to the bathroom."

James stared at me. "Are you sure?"

"I'm not positive of anything, but if I had to bet, I'd bet I'm right." I shoved them back in James's hands. "Go get your money back."

"I can't!"

"You said you'd make good. I just spent three hundred dollars."

"I'll give you your money, but I can't go back on the streets . . . not just yet."

Ozzy interrupted. "We're doing the best we can, Kaida."

I was furious, but I kept my temper in check. "James, you have to go back and ask for antibiotics—that's what we call them—because if these are laxatives, they won't help my friend at all."

James said, "Kaida, the authorities are always looking to get me. I have to be careful."

Ozzy said, "James has already put himself on the line—"

"I realize that, but if he can't buy it, we'll have to get what she needs." I glared at James. "And I need money to do that."

"Here's the money," James said.

I felt bad about coming down on him. "I'm sorry. I know you did the best you could. But this . . . it won't help." I paused. "Here. Take twenty for your help."

James refused the bill. "I feel terrible and I'd go again, but there's no sense in getting arrested."

"You're right. You stay put." I turned to Ozzy. "If we have to relive the accident, it would help to get Joy better first. Her arm's in bad shape. Joy needs something more. If you're getting spills from my world—or copying medicine from where I came from—I can tell what's what. So you need to show me where I can buy the stuff so I can make sure I get the right thing."

"It's too dangerous," James said.

"I don't care," I told him. "I'm not asking you to go, just to tell me where to go."

"I won't let you do it," Ozzy said.

"What do you mean you won't *let* me!" I protested. "I fell into this mess with her. I'm going to fall out of this mess with her. This isn't your business!"

"Too late for that, Hutchenson. I made it my business. We're now in this together."

James was staring at the two of us. "It's my fault. I'll take care of it. Just give me some time."

"I'm sorry, James, but we don't have time." The trip was a day away. I had to help Joy—set her on the right road—before we all attempted to go back to our world. "I'm not leaving until I find her medicine. Tell me where to find it."

Ozzy gave me a hard look. "You can't go alone. You don't realize what you're up against."

"I'm up against my brother, my friends, my parents, the authorities. I'm up against the entire world right now."

"Welcome to our lives," James said.

"Either show me how to get medicine *or* come with me to get medicine." Tears finally sprouted in my eyes. "I'm not saying your help wouldn't be appreciated, but one way or the other, I'm going to get what Joy needs."

James let out a long whistle. "Spitfire."

Dragon-girl was my parents' nickname for me, and the words echoed in my head. I was playing the part of some heroine out of a Manga comic strip. So how come I didn't feel invincible?

Ozzy closed his eyes, then opened them. He whispered. "James can't go out there again. It's like asking him to be eliminated."

"I'm not *asking* him to do it, Ozzy, I'm just asking him to tell me where to go."

"I know you're willing to brave it alone . . . but just like we don't know your world, you don't know ours." He tapped his foot. "I'll come with you, Kaida. I'll make sure you get the right spills. I'll do it."

"I'm not asking you to do it."

"I know that. I *want* to come with you." He took my hand. "I'm going to come whether you want me to or not. I'll show you the ropes."

"That"—I smiled through my tears—"would be lovely."

16

We left Rix Plac without saying another word to anyone. When I got into the truck, I said, " We need to pick up Zeke and Joy."

Ozzy turned on the ignition, again unleashing the wild animals under the hood. "If all goes smoothly, why bother them?"

"And if it doesn't go smoothly, half of us will be in one place and half of us will be somewhere else."

The engine idled. He didn't say anything.

"That would make things difficult," I told him.

"Call them," Ozzy finally conceded. "Tell them to get over here as soon as possible."

"They don't drive," I reminded him. "We have to pick them up."

"Okay, work it out with them. I'm just the chauffeur." Ozzy clapped the dashboard and made a U-turn.

After I made the arrangements, I said, "Zeke's walking over to Joy's house. Her mother is a lot less intrusive than his parents or my parents."

"Fine. This 'no one gets left behind' is a nice idea in theory, but it doesn't always work out."

"It's not even a matter of no one gets left behind. They came in *with* me, Ozzy. They have opinions, too. It's not use 'em and lose 'em when the body mass gets a little heavy."

He raised his eyebrows and accelerated the truck.

"You're one of the good guys," I reminded him. "We need your help. All of us."

He shook his head. "Sometimes I wonder if I'm hurting my mom as much as I'm helping her. She's not getting any worse, but she isn't improving. Maybe I'm getting the wrong spills."

"You know, even where I come from, sometimes people get sick and die and there isn't anything anyone can do about it. Sometimes people get sick and if they're on the right medicine . . . the proper spill . . . they won't get better but they won't get worse. And sometimes people do get better. Nothing is perfect, Ozzy. The difference is back home, we try to do something." I hesitated and then touched his hand. "Here and back home."

He barely smiled, but I think he felt better. We rode in

silence until we arrived in front of Joy's house. They were waiting by the curb, and when they saw us, they hopped in the back part of the cab, which was a little squished for Zeke's long legs.

Joy was clutching her arm.

I immediately gave her what I thought was Advil. When she looked at me, I said, "Don't ask."

She thanked me, and gulped down two tablets. She said, "Where are we going?"

"What we're doing is really dangerous, but it's the only way we can get you the spills you need." Ozzy made a sharp turn. "The area is pretty run down. Don't freak, okay?"

"After what we've been through, freaking isn't in our vocabulary," Zeke said.

"You all should go on without me," Joy whispered. "I'm holding everyone back."

"Stop it," I told her. "One for all and all for one."

"Me, too," Zeke said.

Ozzy said, "I'm in."

"There were only three musketeers," Zeke said.

"There was d'Artagnan," I said.

Ozzy smiled.

But it didn't last long. His expression turned serious and tense as we entered a no-man's zone. He slowed the truck down to a crawl. Night was falling and it was getting darker by the moment. The place reeked of illness and rot.

"Christ!" Joy jumped as a hand slapped the window of the truck. I turned back and saw a skeletal man gaping at me in desperation.

"Don't look out," Ozzy told us.

So of course, we all looked out. The streets that we drove down were filled with broken buildings and tenement slums with bodies darting in and out of the shadows. The few human souls that we could make out barely looked like people—their bodies ripping at the seams. I wished that Ozzy would pick up the speed, and just get it over with, but I suppose when you're doing stuff on the sly, you have to be methodical. He certainly seemed to know what he was looking for.

"Who are these people?" Zeke finally asked.

"They're sick. Ordinarily, they would be picked up and eliminated. They're running from the cleanup crew . . . maybe hoping to score some spills to keep them alive a little longer."

"So why don't the cleanup crews just come in and arrest everyone?" I asked him.

"They make raids—the crews certainly have plants and spies here. That's what I'm nervous about." Ozzy licked his lips. "But there are many more sick people than the crews can eliminate. The crews have to pick and choose, and hopefully they won't choose today to make a raid."

"My God!" The stench was getting to me, and I nearly gagged. "This is nauseating."

"Yeah, it smells pretty bad. Most of the people here are going to die. They just spend the rest of their lives here, wandering around and hoping for a miracle." He glanced sideways at me.

I felt like I was going to cry.

"Whatever happened to death with dignity?" Joy said softly.

"It's better if you don't look," he told us.

"I can't help it." Zeke's voice was choked. "It's like those World War Two films . . . with all those Jews hiding from the Nazis."

Ozzy honked as a woman with a swollen face shuffled in front of us, pressing her face against the windshield. He rolled down the window. "Get away or I'll call the crew!"

She shuffled off.

"That was cold," Zeke told him.

"You want to get us arrested, Anderson?" Ozzy blew out air. "It's all sad. It's all pathetic. Like I said, you've got to pick and choose." He inched up, making an abrupt stop behind a girl with no arms. He honked the horn and the girl got out of his way.

A man came up to my window and pressed his palm against the glass. There was a hole in his hand. I bowed my head and when I looked up a minute later, a spot of blood had marked the window.

Ozzy swung the truck around and parked. "This isn't doing us any good. We need to walk and seek. You guys okay with that?"

"Sure, definitely." I looked out the window and thought, *No, I'm not okay with walking. I'm not even remotely okay with that. How could anyone be okay with that?*

"Great." He turned to Joy and Zeke. "You guys want to wait or do you want to come with us?"

Joy was crying and Zeke pulled her into his arms, but he didn't look too well either. "We're okay." Zeke let out a nervous laugh that sounded like my flute when it's out of tune. "Honest."

"Then let's do it. Ozzy got out of the truck and slammed the door behind him. Someone tapped on my window and I let out a tiny yelp. It was just Ozzy opening the door for me. I exhaled and stepped onto the curb. Zeke followed, with Joy hidden in the folds of his coat. Ozzy put a protective arm around me and we began what seemed like a descent into hell.

If I'd blown on the buildings, they could've fallen down. It stank like one big diseased gutter and looked like your worst nightmare, with rag-doll people limping across the street, flitting about. And the noises they made—agonizing, strained squeals like half-dead animals, barely clinging to a wisp of life.

I rubbed my eyes. What else could I do?

"Can I hook you up, baby?" a skinny woman crooned. She came out of nowhere and shook a few paper bags in front of us. "Is your mama dying? Your friend? You look a little dying yourself, honey!"

"Ignore them," Ozzy stated in a monotone. "They're selling crap."

We walked a bit more, and then Ozzy stopped and gripped my shoulders. "I need to leave you here for a minute."

"*What?*" Zeke said.

"I don't want you going in with me . . . just in case it's a setup."

"It's okay," I broke in. "We can handle it." Once I acted valiant, Zeke had no choice but to posture as well. "Yeah, we'll be okay." I reassured Ozzy with a smile. I looked five paces away at my newfound friends, all of us scarred for life.

"You're sure?"

Not at all. Please don't leave me. Take us back. "Absolutely."

"We're fine," Zeke chimed in.

"I'm not," Joy said. "Just hurry up."

"I will." And then Ozzy disappeared into the inky black.

A voice croaked out, "You're too pretty to die!"

I must have jumped ten feet. A chubby kid who looked no older than twelve gave me a toothless smile. "I've got something for you if you want it."

"Get lost!" Zeke said with a commanding voice.

The kid disappeared.

"You didn't have to shout," Joy said.

"I'm only doing what Ozzy would have done."

Two teenage boys were laughing at us, their bulbous eyes mocking our fear. One of them had a soul patch; the other was clean shaven but had a wart on his nose.

Wart chucked my chin and coughed. "Look at this young-ness. They look ready to go?"

"Beat it!" Zeke told them. But the boys were older and they ignored him.

Soul Patch said, "Look at their hair, those eyes!"

"Bright eyes."

"You may be dying, but we can help."

"Get the hell away from them, you amateur twits!" a deep voice shouted.

I whipped around and saw it wasn't Ozzy, but some bean-pole redhead with freckles and a black T-shirt. Whoever he was, he shooed the teens away.

"You Kaida?" the redhead asked.

"Who wants to know?" I said.

The redhead chuckled, but it wasn't a happy sound. "I got your pain-erase. Look down."

I did. At my feet was a plastic bottle. When I looked back up, the guy was gone. I blinked, and a few tears escaped my eyes. Tears of relief, maybe. I picked up the bottle and sorted through the pills.

"What are those?" Joy asked.

"Hopefully antibiotics." I shook my head. "The last time they sold James—that's Ozzy's friend—what looked to me like laxatives. They told him it would help your arm."

"Laxatives?" Zeke said.

"Obviously, it's an imperfect system. There's as many cheats in spill dealing as there are in drug dealing." From the distance, I saw Ozzy waving at us.

"Hey." Ozzy's voice was tense. "We got it. Let's blow."

And then we all heard it: the awful wailings of sirens getting louder and louder. Flashing red lights burned through the black sky. There must have been a dozen cars.

"Damn!" Ozzy grabbed me and waved to Zeke and Joy. We all began racing back to the truck, but we were too late. Within seconds the streets were filled with a crowd of men in official uniforms.

"This way." Ozzy pulled me behind a building, with Zeke and Joy in tow.

A megaphone blasted out, "Hands up, hands up, hands up!"

I whispered, "Who are they talking to?"

"Whoever they caught," Ozzy said. "Shhhh . . ."

"Individual evaluations here!" the megaphone continued. "If you've got nothing to hide, we have nothing against you."

Another megaphone. "Cooperate, people! It's your only hope."

"Government police," Ozzy said in my ear. "We'll be fine if we just—"

"Stay hidden?" someone said in my other ear.

I could feel his wet lips against my face and I jumped up reflexively. From behind, a man grabbed my arms and smashed my hands together behind my back. Within seconds, I was handcuffed. "And the rest of you!" he snarled at us. "Don't even think about moving!"

Wasting no time, Ozzy lunged at the man and grabbed his head, smashing it against the building. "RUN!"

I tried to run, but without my arms free I couldn't move quickly enough. I turned around and saw that Joy was still crouched, weeping on the ground.

"Joy!" I screamed, "Get out! Zeke! Get her out! Get her out!"

But a beefy cop had already secured Zeke in a headlock. Within seconds, someone grabbed me from behind and yanked me backward. I almost tripped, but I managed to keep upright. My flight to freedom had come to a quick end.

"You're all under arrest!" a voice shouted.

Something blunt and heavy landed on my head.

Then the whole scene disappeared.

17

For as long as I can remember, my perfect way of waking up is with someone gently touching my hair. I opened my eyes and blinked. Colors and shapes danced before my eyes, and I was having trouble focusing. Everything was dark and murky. There was a rumbling beneath me, and I realized I was lying prone in a moving vehicle. How I got there was anyone's guess.

"Hey, honey," a hoarse voice croaked.

It sounded like a guy. "Dad?" I said. My voice was like a gasp.

Different forms of laughter overlapped one another.

"It's Ozzy," a scratchy voice said.

"Ozzy?" I choked. "Ozzy, were you just touching my hair?"

The laughter spilled over again.

"No, honey . . ." The same croaky voice. "I wish I could. I'm cuffed."

Dreams could be treacherous. I blinked again and saw his bruised face, a gash tracing itself from his eye to his chin.

There was more laughter.

"Shut up!" Ozzy muttered under his breath.

"What's going on back there?" a man barked. When Ozzy didn't answer, the man said, "Shut the hell up."

"Wha . . . ?" was all I managed to get out.

"It's okay, Kaida," Ozzy whispered.

It didn't feel okay. "Where are we going?"

He sighed. "Jail."

I shut my eyes. As much as I liked Ozzy and would miss his smile and his voice, I was ready to wake up and have this whole scenario be one hellish dream. So why was I still handcuffed, lying in the back of a van, my head throbbing in pain?

I started to cry, soft sobs that I was trying to stifle.

Ozzy brushed his foot against mine. "I'm going to get us out of—"

"That's it!" someone in the front seat interrupted. "Shut up! Both of you. Not one damn word more, you got it?"

Not one damn word more meant we couldn't even respond.

More than anything—more than wanting to go home or wanting the pain to stop—more than anything I wanted sleep. Sleep seemed like the only plausible solution in my grasp. And if I forgot about everything enough—forgot about how our cuts and gashes would probably get infected, forgot about how we'd probably rot away in some corrupt prison, and forgot about how this could very well likely be the end . . . well, then sleep wasn't too difficult at all.

I willed myself to close my eyes. A few moments later, I felt my consciousness drifting away until someone had opened the rear doors and light was shining into my eyes. Again the rude awakening.

"All right, delinquents," said one of the cops. "Up you go like good little ones."

The other cop snorted. I think he was the driver. "We've arrived at your new place of residence."

"Cheer up," the first one said to us. "You two look like you have some rich mommies and daddies to bail you out of jail."

The driver chuckled. "Bail? There isn't going to be any bail for this one." He was referring to Ozzy, I think. "Spill-dealing, resisting arrest, assault of an officer—you got three marks against you. And this little witch isn't much better."

"I'm only fifteen!" I gasped.

"Did I say speak?" the driver barked back. "Fifteen doesn't mean nothing. Fifteen means you're a young criminal instead of an old criminal."

"But we're minors," I protested.

"What the hell is she saying, Marty?"

"Not a clue, Simon." Marty yanked Ozzy out of the car. The other man grabbed me and pulled me out and onto the sidewalk.

It was a strange time to feel weightless.

"We got ourselves Romeo and Juliet here," Simon told Marty in a mocking, overly sweet voice. "Getting themselves into all sorts of trouble."

I wondered if, in this world, the play would include the part about the poison and the antidote? If only the characters hadn't been so impulsive. If only they'd had someone to stop them. Their friends, maybe? Their friends . . .

"Joy." I coughed. "Zeke."

"Shut up," said Simon. "You dunno what the hell you're saying."

"You'll have plenty of time to talk to your Romeo," Marty growled.

The dynamic duo of Marty and Simon shuffled us like cattle into an ugly building that was peopled with men who doubled as gargoyles. It didn't look like any police station I'd ever seen. There were no desks anywhere, just nasty-looking drones sitting in folding chairs, drinking beer and smoking. My head hurt and my shoulders ached from having my hands cuffed behind my back. I didn't know what my face looked like, but it had to be better than Ozzy's.

Someone opened a door from the main room, and the

two cops shoved us inside. They walked us through a series of ocher-painted hallways with closed doors on either side. Marty finally found a door he liked and unlocked it. He took the cuffs off of Ozzy and threw him into what seemed like a windowless closet.

"Enjoy the last bits of light because you're not seeing anything for a while."

From behind I felt my handcuffs loosen. Simon turned to Marty. "Sure you don't want them cuffed?"

"No need. There's no chance in hell they'll get out."

The door closed, and once again I was surrounded by strangling darkness just like in the cave. I had come out of one pitch-black hell to find myself, again, in a bleak, sightless void.

"It's okay," Ozzy mumbled into my ear. "We'll get out of this . . . somehow!"

Then I thought of something. "Our one phone call," I reminded him. "Don't we—"

"You watch too much television," he said. "When it comes to spill dealers, they don't really care whether we live or not."

"We're not spill dealers," I said wryly. "We're spill buyers."

He kissed my nose. "I was aiming for your cheek. Can't really see where I'm aiming."

"I can't see anything either." I felt hopeless. No light and no space.

"There's a crack at the bottom of the door," he pointed out. "I'm going to sit up, okay?"

"Okay, let me just . . ."

I flopped over like a dead fish. My senses seemed to all kick in at the same time, and suddenly I was smelling the fetid stink of the room. The floors were sticky and the walls were uneven. I sucked in air and then immediately regretted it.

I could make out a sliver of yellow at the bottom of the door. "Oh, thank God, you beautiful little crack of light!"

"The crack?" a voice grumbled from outside. "The crack's no more."

And suddenly it was gone. Our one source of light, our one slice of sanity, had disappeared. They must've put a towel or something in front of the door.

"Shit," Ozzy swore. Any hope he was holding on to had faded from his voice. We were both fatally screwed.

My voice trembled as I spoke. "Our parents will come."

"I don't know where the hell we are, Kaida. Your parents might look for you, but the guys here are corrupt. They don't want us out. Eventually your parents will probably assume something bad happened, and that'll be that."

I bit my lip. I'd never heard anything so fatalistic.

"So you think they're just going to figure I'm dead and leave it at that?"

"Where you are now, that's not that strange." Ozzy exhaled. "We were driving for a long time. I don't know where they've taken us. We could be hundreds of miles from where you live. And there's no way my mother will be able to look for me. She can barely . . ." His voice drifted off. "I don't know what to do, Kaida. I'm sorry."

"No, I'm sorry." Here was the part where the tears came in buckets. "I dragged you into this."

"No, I dragged you into this."

"We can't both be the dragger. Someone has to be the draggee."

We twisted and tangled until we were facing each other. I couldn't see him, but I could feel his breath, the only thing that smelled human. He put his hands on my shoulders and pulled me to him until our noses were touching.

I had kissed people before and it had been fun: worry-free stuff by public pools. One time it was after French Club by the parking lot. Those moments hadn't been especially passionate or especially enjoyable. But they hadn't been rushed, frantic touches emerging out of despair.

For what it was worth, I decided this time was better.

"Kaida?" he whispered in my ear.

"What?" I felt a hum spreading from my ear to my neck.

"I'm going to get us out of this mess."

I rested my head on his chest. He ran his fingers through my hair and down my spine.

"Are you crying?" he asked.

"No," I lied.

"You're crying." He kissed the top of my head. "I can feel it."

"Ozzy, how many girlfriends have you had?"

He stroked my hair. "I can't believe you're thinking about that right now."

"A lot, right?" I persisted.

"No, not a lot." He chuckled. "And I've never had a girl-friend named Kaida with whom I got arrested."

"We need to get out of here," I stated.

"Yes," he agreed. "Any ideas? I'm certainly open."

My eyes flicked around, unable to adjust to the blackness. "We should both just think about it."

"Good idea." He lay down and pulled me on top of him. I rested my head on his chest, turning it sideways. With one hand, he walked his fingers up and down my back, giving me the chills. The movements became slower until they stopped and I rose and fell with each of Ozzy's breaths.

"Snack time!" a voice boomed.

My body was jolted awake.

I hadn't slept long enough to forget where I was, nor did I feel any better about it.

Something clicked and popped and then the door opened. A paunchy guy in what looked like yellow pajamas held a tray. "You can eat it with the lights off alone." He switched on the electricity. "Or you can eat with the lights on under my supervision."

With the room lit up, its true repulsiveness was finally illuminated.

"What'll it be?"

"Lights on." Ozzy was still lying on the floor.

"Lights on for me, too," I told him. Anything was better than suffocating blackness.

"You got it, chickadee." The man seemed more cheerful than the other two had been. When you get yourself in a bad way, you learn to count your pluses. He entered the room and closed the door, ducking because the ceiling was so low. Miraculously, he managed to sit in such a confining space.

"We got biscuits, crackers, jam, and some lukewarm tea," the man said. "I can get you extra if you want."

"Thank you very much." I was shocked by the humane treatment we were getting.

Ozzy said, "Thank you, sir."

"It's Officer Maurice." He added, "I also brought a couple cans of soda."

"Thanks." Ozzy sat up. "Thanks a lot, Officer. We really appreciate it."

"Anything else I can get you kids?" Maurice offered.

The truth is, there was a lot he could get us, thank you very much, but nothing we were stupid enough to ask for. I shook my head.

"This is fine, thank you."

Ozzy sneaked a sidelong glance at me. He was as mystified as I was. Maurice set the tray down on the floor. I picked up a plastic knife and slathered jam on my biscuit. Ozzy followed suit.

We ate everything on the tray. Maurice just kept smiling like we were old chums dining out after a high-school basketball game. When we were finished, he again offered us anything we wanted.

"I think I'm okay."

Ozzy nodded. "Thank you."

A smile slipped from Maurice's lips. He rubbed the side of his face. Picking up the tray, he attempted to get up, but couldn't do so without opening the door. "If you need some more grub, just knock."

"Thanks so much," I said. My voice was absolutely dripping with gratitude.

When he closed the door, he did it gently. Again we were encased in darkness.

I said, "What was that all about?"

"He was treating us like jailhouse royalty," Ozzy said. "Not that I'm complaining." He burped. "Man, that stuff's even worse coming up."

"At least we're full."

"I hope he didn't poison us."

"God, I hope not." I slid into his open arms. "If so, it's been nice knowing you."

"Ditto."

"He seemed genuinely nice." I waited a beat. "Could be wishful thinking. At least it's easier to think on a full stomach. I wonder where Joy and Zeke are."

"No idea."

"If we are going to re-create the exact-same scenario as

the accident, we'll need them."

"Right now, Kaida, our brains need to be thinking about the present and not the future."

"Agreed."

We thought and thought and thought.

We thought ourselves to sleep.

18

When I was little, I used to rub my hands against my closed eyes to see what colors would pop into my brain. I'd get a headache afterward, and I was never sure that a few seconds of kaleidoscopic images were worth the pain. But in jail those patterns were the only ones I could see, and even those came in dark colors.

We were trying to fall sleep again—there was nothing else to do—but my circuitry was still running at full speed. "Ozzy?"

"Wha . . ."

"We need to get out of here," I said for the fiftieth time.

". . . kay."

At least one of us was resting. It was all right, though, sort of peaceful lying beside each other in a closet without light or ventilation or sheets and a pillow.

Or a bathroom.

My stomach lurched, churning as if to say, "Yup! No bathroom! That's right, babe!" The snack may have been the last straw for my overworked, nervous stomach.

"Oh, God," I said quietly, clutching my belly.

"Mm," Ozzy hummed.

My intestines were performing acrobatics. I jumped up, hitting my head on the ceiling. "Damn!" I pounded on the door. "I need a bathroom! I need a bathroom! I need a—"

"One second!" a muffled voice called back.

The door swung open and Maurice was there, this time dressed in bright orange scrubs.

"I need a bathroom."

"No problem. Follow me."

I turned to Ozzy. "I'll be back."

We began to walk, but almost immediately I tripped and fell facedown. There was too much light, and I was already cramped all over in pain.

Maurice helped me up with his meaty palms. "Can you walk?"

I had erupted into a cold sweat. "With help."

"Lean on me."

I did. He took me down a flight of stairs and into a hallway, passing a few doors before he opened one of them. Inside it was clean and white.

"This is my bathroom, darling," he said gently.

"Thank you so much!" Despite my sore limbs, I nearly leaped out of his arms.

The next twenty minutes weren't fun.

When I came out, Maurice was waiting for me.

"Anything else you need?" he offered.

I thought about it. What did we have to lose? I could say no and sit in a closet with Ozzy for the next thirty years or I could be honest. He seemed decent enough, although he could just be fattening me up for the slaughter. But even if he was, things couldn't get much worse.

"Yes, there is something."

Maurice raised his bushy gray eyebrows. *Yes* clearly wasn't the predicted response.

"Help me find my friends and help me get home."

There was a long, long pause. I felt I'd blown it.

Finally he said, "Who are your friends?"

My heart was beating so fast I could barely talk. "Joy Tallon and Zeke Anderson."

"How can I help you get home?" His eyes met mine. "I can't even get myself home."

I tilted my head to one side. "Don't you guys ever get a break?"

He smiled sadly. "I need to get you back."

There was something about his face that captivated me: his droopy brown eyes, his sad, speckled nose, his glistening forehead marked by a scar.

It was a captivating scar, and I couldn't figure out why. Then it dawned on me.

There had been stitches holding the seams together at one point.

"No!" I gasped, nearly keeling over again. I could count them: six neat parallel hash marks over a crooked line. "You're not from here, either!"

Maurice's eyes got wide. He let out a laugh, but it was tinged with anxiety. "I think the darkness got to your brain. Let's get you back."

I pointed to my forehead. Then I pointed to his. "You have stitches," I whispered.

The hesitation was minuscule, and I caught it only because I was looking for it. "Stitches?" he said. "What are those?"

"You know what I'm saying—"

"No, I don't. Look, little one, you're a kid and I feel sorry for you, but—"

"You come from where I come from," I interrupted him. "Where there are doctors and nurses and hospitals and medicine and cures, and where spills aren't illegal!"

He grabbed my arm. "You have to whisper!"

I nodded feverishly. I don't know what came over me . . . to talk so freely. I guess it just came out in an uncontrollable rush.

He loosened his grip. "I don't . . . ." He faltered. "It can't be."

"I came through a cave," I told him. "How did you get here?"

He screwed up his face, like he was really thinking about it, but then his eyes got hard and his mouth set in a stony frown. "Back to your room!" He led me by the nape of my neck.

"Ow!" I cried.

"Enough out of you!" He led me back up to the closet and carelessly threw me on top of a dozing Ozzy.

"Shit," I swore as Maurice slammed the door.

"Ye Gods," Ozzy gasped while wrapping his arms around me. "Are you all right, Kaida?"

"He comes from where I come from," I answered breathily. I still felt his fingers digging into the nape of my neck. The pain had trickled down to my sore shoulders.

"What?" Ozzy tried to sit up while still holding on to me. It took a few moments. "What are you talking about?"

"Maurice. He's from my world."

"Are you sure?"

"I'm positive. He's scared to admit it. That's why he was so nice to us. He knows about medicine, so he's probably sympathetic to spill dealers."

Ozzy's grip around me tightened reflexively. "Why would he be working here?"

"I don't know." I felt defeated, as if my one chance had been blown sky high. My eyes watered. "Maurice is the only decent human being we've encountered in the last six hours, and now he's lost to us because of my loose lips."

211

"Nah . . ." Ozzy brushed it off. "They're all beasts. They're all corrupt. I'm sure Maurice is just like the rest of them."

I was panting. "We need to find some way to get him to realize that we're not the enemy. We've got to get him on our side!"

"That, my dear, is impossible."

"He sympathizes with us, Ozzy. I know he does. It's just that he can't admit it."

"How do you know he's from your world?"

"He had markings on his forehead . . . stitches. Do you know what stitches are?"

"No."

After I explained it to him, he didn't answer.

Then he said, "I'm nodding, Kaida, but I guess you can't see."

"Look, he has to give us another meal, right?" I reasoned.

"Yeah, someone has to. It might not be him." The room turned deathly still. "If he's scared of us finding out the truth, maybe he won't be our guardian angel anymore."

I thought about it. It depended on whether or not the guy had any conscience. Tricky.

I thought about calling him back, but I was afraid it was too soon.

There was nothing we could do right now.

The closet remained silent, both of us feeling too hopeless to talk.

It must have been only a half hour later when the door opened and a beam of light shot into the cell. I held my hands over my eyes.

"How did *you* get here?"

The voice was almost inaudible.

I thought: *You should know how I got in this damn cell. You're the police.*

But when I looked through my fingers, I saw Maurice.

The meaning of the question shifted entirely.

I went out alone with him, leaving Ozzy and a part of my heart behind. Maurice took me to a private room and closed the door. We sat with the lights out so as not to attract attention. It felt good to sit on a chair, albeit a steel one. At least it was a surface that wasn't coated with muck. I told him my story. Then he asked me to repeat it. I gave him a summary this time: the trip, the accident, the storm, and finally the cave.

"I fell in through a cave."

I could feel his breath on my face. It smelled like cigar smoke, not very pleasant but much better than the room I had been in.

"Actually, I got lost in a cave and fell into a pit. When I woke up, I was in my own room. Everything looked the same . . . but it wasn't. The entire field of medicine had been wiped away from the face of the earth."

It took a long time for Maurice to speak. Then he said,

"I'm going to tell you a story. It may be true, but it may not be true, get it?"

"I understand." I paused as my ears perked up. "What's that?"

"What's what?"

"I heard something." We stopped talking, but the sound had disappeared. *Cease the paranoia, Kaida.* "I'm nervous."

"You don't trust me, kid?"

I didn't answer.

"Being suspicious is being smart. What was I saying?"

"You were going to tell me a story."

"That's right." He cleared his throat. "One day a man was hiking. It began to rain and he also took shelter in a cave. The storm got very bad, so bad that he had to back into the cave a little farther to keep from getting wet. It was dark, it was muddy. He didn't see too well. And then all of a sudden he fell into a puddle." He paused. "Not in a puddle, into a puddle."

"A puddle that wasn't a puddle."

"Yes, exactly."

Maurice finally said, "What about your boyfriend?"

"He's from here . . . from this world," I answered. There was no reason to trust Maurice, but I figured I didn't have too much too lose. "He's a spill dealer with a very sick mother. He was getting some medic—some spills for my friend. That's why we're here."

"And your friends—what about them?"

"Also from my world." I waited a beat. "*Our* world."

"I want to help you, Kaida, but I don't know what I can do."

You could do a lot . . . like getting me out of here. But it was important not to rush things. "I'm sorry if this is personal, but how did you end up working here?"

Maurice's voice was a hush. "I started as a dealer. When I got caught by the cops, I panicked and told them everything. About where I came from and how I didn't belong." He paused. "It was just the kind of information they wanted, those jerks. They kept me around to interrogate me. It started out as weeks, then it was months, then it lasted for more than a year. They asked me question after question until I dried up. When I ran out of information, they decided to use me as a jail guard . . . you know, to keep an eye on me. Better that they watch the enemy than have me running around loose."

"Why didn't they just kill you?"

"Good question." Maurice paused. "There's a woman who studies people like me. She's a full professor with a lot of grants."

"Iona Boyd," I said.

"So you know."

"Ozzy does research for her."

"Tell him to watch his back. She's not what she seems. She has a lot of clout because she's married to someone who's high up in the government in covert investigations."

"Like the CIA?"

215

"Something like that. The point is Iona Boyd was one of the people who interrogated me. She learns things from people like us."

"I know about the testimonials," I told him.

"That's just the tip of the iceberg." He sighed. "And did you ever wonder what happened to those people?"

"I hadn't, but I was wondering now."

Maurice said, "I'm a prisoner here, one with a nice office, but I don't have any freedom. I have no home, I live here. I stay here, day in and day out, doing dirty work."

I had to tell Ozzy about Iona Boyd. As I thought of him, my heart leaped in my chest. "Maurice, why are these people so opposed to the concept of health care?"

"Because they're cowards and hypocrites!" He snorted quietly. "They kept accusing me—accusing spill-dealers—of trying to change the natural order . . . that we're tampering with the natural ebb and flow of the earth."

It sounded like a theory that could have come from my world.

"But they don't believe a word of that," he growled. "The government agents take care of themselves. Iona Boyd makes sure of that."

"What do you mean?" I asked.

"She uses the information that she's learned from us for the select few, Kaida." An angry grunt. "They all have secret spills and their own personal spill dealer. They have spills to help them get better, but just for themselves and for their families.

They're just too greedy to share them. It makes them powerful. It makes them strong and leaves the rest of us weaklings
to die from neglect."

"There is some minimal form of health care," I said.
"People still shower and wash their face and brush their teeth
and dry them with a tooth rag."

He let out a quiet but wry "Ha!" "They want their society
not to stink. Odor offends all of us."

I tapped my fingers against my leg. "Maurice, do you want
to get out of this world?"

"Of course." His voice was choked up. "Of course I do.
But I don't know *how*!"

The next few pleas came out in a hot rush. This might
have been my last chance to beg. "Then help us escape. My
class is going on a trip to the same caves that we were visiting
before we fell down the pit. Maybe if Joy, Zeke, and I go back
on the trip, maybe, just *maybe,* everything will happen again.
The crash, getting lost in the desert, the storm, escaping to the
cave, falling down into the pit, running to the light and then
falling . . . maybe we can go back to where we came from!"

"And what if it doesn't happen?" Maurice's voice quavered.
"What if you just crash and die?"

"It couldn't be much worse than this." When he didn't
answer, I said, "The sooner you get us out, the closer we can
come to finding a link, however faint, between these two
places. And if we do discover that door, maybe we can bring
you back."

"But how?"

"I'm not sure. But isn't it worth a try?"

Maurice touched the scar on his forehead. "It's more complicated than you think, Kaida. The government has people working everywhere. Anyone you know could be a member of the secret police. Hell, they might be watching us right now. You could have been sent here to frame me."

"Then we'll have to be quick."

"I'm not sure there's enough time to get you out without arousing suspicion," Maurice said.

"At least show me where Zeke and Joy are. Maybe they'll have some ideas."

"Too risky."

I paused, trying to think up a plan to convince him that I was his only hope. I figured the only way to get him to stop worrying about himself was to make him worry about something else.

I said, "Maurice, you have all the power. You don't need to help us, I know. You're safe even if we're not. I could sit here forever in prison rotting. And no doubt I will rot, considering what this society believes about health. Maybe that was the idea of putting me in the closet in the first place. So guards could have fun watching us rot."

No one said anything for what appeared to be the longest time. Then he spoke. "What were the names of your friends again?"

"Zeke Anderson and Joy Tallon," I told him. "T-A-L-L-O-N."

"Wait here."

"Okay."

As if I had any choice. He patted my head and left. As soon as I was alone, tears filled my eyes. I cried for what I had and lost. I cried for my parents and brother and friends. I cried for Ozzy and his sick mother. I cried and cried until I couldn't cry anymore. Maurice was my last chance, and if I lost him, I lost myself.

When I finally had sniffed my last sniff, my eyes closed and I fell asleep on the chair until I woke up with a crick in my neck. Maurice still hadn't returned, so I dropped to the floor, curled up in the fetal position, and closed my eyes. I slept the sleep of the dead.

I was awakened by the sound of a door opening. Maurice had returned with another guard in tow.

"Get up," he said gruffly.

I wiped the light from my aching eyes and recognized the second guard as Simon. I stood and said nothing.

"We're transporting you," Maurice said officiously. "Making room for delinquents worse than you."

"Pretty hard to find," Simon told us, "but we found 'em."

They took me down a long corridor with barred cells on either side. This area looked like the jails I'd seen on TV. The walls were the same ocher yellow and the floors were sticky plastic tiles. I couldn't tell whether it was day or night because there were no windows anywhere and the lighting was artificial: casino time, my dad used to call it whenever he went to Las Vegas. Inside Sin City, there is no sense of the passage of time.

Most of the inmates were sleeping on steel cots in spaces about as big as the closet we had been in. There was no privacy. Truly it was life in a fishbowl. I didn't know what was worse—continuous light or nothing but darkness. Probably the latter. At least with light, you can close your eyes.

A few minutes later, Maurice told Simon that he could handle me alone. To my eyes, it appeared that not exerting himself with work made Simon almost as happy as harassing me. After he left, Maurice started unlocking a cell door. Apparently Zeke and Joy hadn't been thrown in a black hole, because they hadn't punched the cops or tried to escape. Still, their accommodations were far from deluxe. The cell was bigger—room enough for four with four steel cots plus one sink and one toilet.

Going to the bathroom in front of one another. Disgusting!

"Kaida?" Joy choked when she saw me. She was curled next to Zeke. No blankets, but they did have a couple of burlap potato sacks for pillows. "Is this a dream?"

I put my finger to my lips to shush her. They had formed a smile. I couldn't help it. When this whole thing had started,

220

I didn't really care about Joy. Now I regarded her as a blood sister.

Although to me it seemed like only a night had passed, Joy looked like she had been starved and beaten for weeks. Her eyes were sunken with bluish circles smudged under them. "Were you sleeping?" I whispered.

She shook her head. "I haven't slept at all. Her dark eyes smoldered, saying: *How could I sleep?*

I looked over at Maurice, who was still unlocking the cell. The lock was incredibly complicated, with slots and buttons, and I almost admired the security of the prison.

"Zeke." Joy shook him gently. "Zekey?"

Nothing like enforced closeness to bring two people together.

Zeke opened an eye, and it focused on me for a few seconds. Then both his eyes widened, and he shot up like a coiled spring. "Kay!—"

"Shhh!" Joy and I silenced him simultaneously.

He looked around and noticed Maurice. His eyes said: *What's going on?*

My eyes replied. *Trust me one more time.*

19

In a bad situation, it's sometimes safer to depend on yourself.
Using your own wits makes you self-sufficient, but self-reliance
can only carry you so far. Sometimes you need a friend telling
you it's going to be all right. Even if, in your heart of hearts,
you're not sure the person is telling the truth.

Or you're not even sure what the truth is.

Maurice was the first *adult* who knew what I was talking
about. I wanted him to pat my hand and tell us that he had
come from our place to get us out of this mess—that that was
his purpose in life. But he remained professional as ever.

"Done!" Maurice swung the cell open. Joy got up once

and fell. Zeke helped her up, but he, too, looked a bit woozy. I wondered if they had been sedated with alcohol. It seemed to be the only depressant that was readily available. At first glance, this place seemed like a party town—smoking and drinking and weed. It reminded me of that saying: Be careful what you wish for.

"What's going on?" a voice growled from one of the other cages.

"None of your business!" Maurice snapped back. "Shut up or I'll extend your stay in Hotel Happiness." He turned to me, his voice almost inaudible. "We need to get Callahan before they catch wind of something."

Maurice pushed the three of us forward. He opened a gray door that led into a poorly illuminated hallway with flickering yellow lights. The ceiling was so low that Zeke had to duck so as not to hit his head. There were periodic video cameras and I wondered how they operated with such little light.

The hallway kept shrinking. There were doors on either side but as the foyer's ceiling became lower, the doors got shorter. I kept expecting them to open up and people from the cleanup crew to pop out in their gleaming white coats. I shivered as I thought of that man being tossed inside a van . . . the remnants of a severed life.

We were walking very fast, but it was hard to see more than a few feet in front of our eyes, like walking in an amber fog.

"Kaida?" Joy's voice rustled.

"Quiet!" Maurice snapped. "Or I'll handcuff you and throw you back in the cage."

I turned around and looked at Joy, trying to be reassuring. Zeke was dragging her forward. Otherwise there was no way that she could have walked that quickly. When we reached the end of the corridor, Maurice opened another door, shoved us inside, and plunged us into darkness once he closed the door.

"No!" Joy yelped. "Not the cave, not the—"

"Shhh!" I sounded harsher than I felt, but now was not the time for freak-outs. "It's not the cave."

"Shut up!" Maurice barked. "This is a service hall, and the video cameras don't work in the dark," he told us. "Use the wall as your guide."

Joy was hyperventilating. "It's all because of me."

I snapped, "It's because of the cave, Joy, not you."

"If it wasn't for you or Zeke, I'd be dead."

"Shhh." Zeke silenced her. "Everyone's fine, Joy."

We walked quickly and clumsily, groping our way through the darkness. We couldn't even see a millimeter in front of us. The wall was sticky, as if years of grease and grime had settled upon it, but it was all we had.

"This way leads to the back entry to where you were," Maurice told me. "Shortcut to your old living quarters. Hopefully, one of the other guards didn't transfer Callahan somewhere else while you were gone."

We continued to fumble along for another five to ten minutes. Finally Maurice told us to stop. He said, "This is the back door to your closet. Wake up, Callahan, so we can get out of here."

I had come full circle, back to the isolated room. There was minimal light in the cell coming from underneath the door in the opposite hallway. Someone must have removed the towel. I could barely make out Ozzy's sprawled-out body. He looked like a corpse, and an involuntary spasm shook my body.

"Ozzy?" I kneeled down and touched his face. He opened his eyes. "Get up. We're leaving."

He rubbed his eyes. "Leaving?"

"You said think of a plan. I thought of a plan. Let's get out of here."

He bolted up and smiled. "Music to my ears."

Maurice must have been serious about escaping with us because he had what looked like a stack of official papers. He handcuffed all of us and marched us to the entrance of the stationhouse. We watched anxiously as he convinced the cops or guards or whoever they were that he was transporting us to another division.

"You got too many prisoners," one of the uniformed guards told him.

"Simon's meeting me outside," Maurice told them.

"He is?" The cop looked slightly bored. "He didn't sign out."

"Want me to have him come in?"

The cop thought about it and shrugged. "You sign him out. If there's a problem, the shit will come down on you. Lemme see your tag."

Maurice lifted up his pants leg and revealed a remote electronic ID ankle bracelet. "If you need me, just buzz."

"Go." The cop waved him along.

Fifteen minutes later, in breaking daylight, the four of us were crammed into the backseat of a police car. We sat behind a metal grate with our hands still cuffed behind our backs. Maurice got in the driver's seat and started the engine, and within moments we were on our way to somewhere.

"What's next?" I asked him.

"First I gotta get rid of this thing."

I knew he was referring to the ankle tag. We drove for ten minutes; then he pulled over to the side.

"It's taken me two years to finally figure out how to get this thing on and off without an alarm going off . . . unless they changed the electronics. Hold your breaths."

We did. Time ticked slowly as he removed the bracelet.

"The moment of truth."

No one moved except Maurice.

"Done!" He rolled down the window and tossed it down a sewer. He was all smiles. "Phew! That was step one. Step two is to get out of this district before the bosses discover that the documents were forged."

"What day is it?" Zeke asked.

"Wednesday."

"What date?"

Maurice told him the date. Zeke gasped.

"What?"

"It's the day of our trip," I said. "You've got to take us to Buchanan High, Maurice. It's our only chance to get back."

He scratched his chin. "When do you have to get there by?"

"We're leaving at nine in the morning," Zeke said. "What time is it now?"

"Around six."

Joy groaned.

"Oh, my God!" I shrieked. "How far are we from the high school?"

He told me an area that didn't sound familiar to any of us except Ozzy, who spoke up. "Do you know where the St. Mark's district is?"

Maurice said, "That's north of Calverson and east of Dunquest."

"Exactly," Ozzy replied. "Can you get us there?"

"If you give me good directions."

And we were off. Again I asked how far we were from Buchanan. Maurice told us we were about two hours away. Suddenly each second began to tick too quickly.

"That went really smoothly," Ozzy said.

"What?" Maurice asked.

"The escape."

"You think it was easy?"

No one spoke.

"The only reason it worked so well is me!" Maurice said. "I've been working at that goddamn station for years, doing whatever those monsters told me to do. I've earned their respect with blood, sweat, and tears."

We gave a collective "thank you." But something was eating at me. The whole situation just didn't seem right. I wanted to ask him why he was doing this, putting himself on the line, but I was too scared. I tapped my feet nervously against the police car's floor.

"I'll get you kids back to school in a couple of hours." With a push of a button, Maurice lowered the grate that separated the front and back seats. "You'll make your trip."

Again I thought about how it was too easy. But I was too afraid to question. "When do we get the cuffs off?"

"Oh . . ." Maurice reached into his pocket, pulled out a ring of keys, and threw them into Ozzy's lap. "Use the small keys. I don't know which is which. I'd pull over to help you, but I don't want to waste time. We need to get out of here."

Was he really on the level? He seemed nervous. He kept checking over his shoulder. I glanced in the rearview mirror. With each moment that passed, his eyes became more wild. Ozzy worked the keys into his handcuffs. It took some time, but finally his hands were free. He shook them out, and it was the first time I'd seen any of us smile in a very long time.

One by one, Ozzy liberated our hands. It felt so good to see my fingers. Joy had been dozing on and off. Once the cuffs were off, she seemed to perk up, although she was still woozy.

In her daze, she asked, "Why are you doing this for us?"

Maurice said, "I'm doing for you what I wish someone would have done for me. I'm doing it because I'm not going back there anymore. You gave me courage to do something I should have done a long time ago. Now don't talk anymore. Save your strength. You'll need it."

I looked out the window while the sky blossomed into pinks and golds. Maurice made a series of turns. He was still looking over his shoulder or in the mirrors every few minutes. I felt my eyes closing, although I didn't want to succumb. I needed to think! I needed to stay awake. But the rhythm . . .

I was jolted awake by a sharp left turn.

"Damn it!" Maurice cried out as he accelerated into a sharp turn. "Hold on, kids, we're going on a ride."

The car shook as Maurice pressed the gas pedal and shot us forward. Suddenly everything was at time-warp speed. Joy and I screamed.

"What the hell is going on?" Zeke exclaimed.

"The Higher Rank!" Maurice cried out. "The goddamned Higher Rank is behind us!"

Sirens blared as the car whooshed at breakneck speed. Two cop cars were on our tail, the strobe lights blinking on top of the vehicles. Maurice shouted, "All of you, duck!"

We fell to the floor. My stomach dropped and suddenly I

knew what must have happened. It had to do with the "nothing" sound that I had heard while Maurice and I had been talking. I looked up and peeked over the seat.

"Get down!"

I obeyed, but I managed to spy in the rearview mirror. Beads of sweat were raining down his forehead.

The sirens kept blaring.

"I think someone overheard our conversation," I said.

"Can't be! Room is soundproof. I did it myself."

But his voice sounded shaky.

"What's the Higher Rank?" Zeke shouted over the roar of the engine.

"The bastards sent to catch people like us," Ozzy told us. "In other words, they're sent out to catch the 'biggest threats to society.'"

"We're done," Maurice barked. "Car won't go any faster." Suddenly he pulled off the road, down an embankment. The car jumped and leaped as we all screamed. I thought for sure that we were going to roll and roll and burst into fire just like the first accident. But this time we were luckier.

Maurice drove like a pro, bouncing the police car along the uneven ground, manipulating the wheels around trees and bushes until he drove into a copse of shrubbery. He slammed on the brakes, throwing everyone forward.

"They're after me, guys. I'll go back up to the road and try to distract them . . . tell them you hijacked me and point them in the wrong direction. Wait until the commotion dies down. Go straight and you'll find a service road. That'll lead you to the highway."

I cried out, "But—"

"Make or break time." Maurice had already unbuckled himself. "Good luck and wish me luck."

He opened the door and jumped out of the car. The last we saw, he was running toward the highway, waving his arms like a traffic cop.

We sat without talking. We were utterly alone.

I turned to Joy. "How's your arm?"

"Hurts, but it hurt before. I think the infection is getting worse."

"Ozzy, can you drive?"

"Yeah, but I don't know where I am or where the hell I should go." Ozzy climbed over the seat and slid into the driver's side. "How long should we wait?"

"The sirens have stopped," I said. "I'm too scared to go out and look."

"Patience," Ozzy said. "Can't rush this."

"We can't wait too long," Zeke said. "We'll miss our trip."

"Better to miss the trip than to go back to jail," I told him, although I really didn't know what was worse: incarceration or being stuck in this universe.

The sirens kicked up again. We listened for a few moments and this time they seemed to be receding into the background.

The Doppler effect. I remembered that from junior-high science.

We remained in our hiding place for another five minutes or so.

Finally Zeke said, "How about getting us back on the main road?"

Ozzy put the car in reverse and swung it around. "I can do that provided . . ."

"What?"

"Provided that the Higher Rank is gone. What if they're still out there looking for us?"

No one answered.

"We won't get anywhere sitting in this ditch." I climbed into the front passenger seat. "We have to believe Maurice . . . that he did what he said he was going to do."

"What if he didn't?" Joy asked.

"We've got to do something," I said. "Inaction is the same thing as giving up."

"Agreed." Ozzy started the engine and we crawled onto the service road. Once we hit the thoroughfare, Ozzy pressed the pedal and accelerated into the flow of traffic until we were doing around eighty.

"You okay back there, Joy?" I asked.

"I'm coping."

I glanced at my wrist to check the time, but I wasn't wearing a watch. Outside the windshield, the sun was rising in a blue sky smudged with white smears. Ozzy drove quickly and efficiently for the next half hour until we were interrupted by another siren.

"Crap," Ozzy swore under his breath, and accelerated. "They caught back up with us . . . the Higher Rank." The speedometer needle was grazing 100 MPH. "Kaida, how many cop cars are there?"

I turned around. No cop cars, just a white van closing in on our bumper.

I looked in the rearview mirror. Saw people in white with flat faces.

It wasn't the Higher Rank.

It was the cleanup crew.

20

"Why are they chasing us?" I asked Ozzy. I was breathless! "We haven't crashed. What do they want with us?"

"I don't know!" Ozzy shouted as he weaved in and out of lanes. "Are they still on our tail?"

"Right behind us!" Joy yelled.

"This is *not* good!" Ozzy let out a deep breath. "Hold on, everyone. If you've never prayed before, maybe now's a good time to start."

He yanked the wheel to the right and swerved across the four-lane highway, exiting onto a service road. I turned around and couldn't see the van, but I could hear the sirens wailing.

Zeke was acting as the lookout, his body turned around so he could see out of the back windshield. "I think they got off the highway."

Ozzy let up on the pedal, then floored it. The car flew forward as Ozzy twisted between cars, passing slowpoke drivers on the right and on the left. All of us shrieked when we nearly collided with an oncoming bus.

"I'd rather be in prison than dead!" Zeke screamed.

"If the cleanup crew catches us, we're as good as dead!" Ozzy yelled back. "Where are they?"

"I can't see them," Zeke said, "but I sure as hell hear them."

Indeed, the air resonated with an ominous *wee-oo, wee-oo, wee-oo*! I remembered the Sirens from the *Odyssey*. They were supposed to kill you by seduction, not by naked terror.

"Move it, move it, move it!" I told Ozzy.

"We're going as fast as we can," he snapped back. "I'm already overheating."

Wee-oo, wee-oo, wee-oo!

"Are they gaining on us?" Ozzy cried out.

"I can't tell," Zeke said.

"What do you see?"

"Commotion."

Wee-oo, wee-oo, wee-oo!

"What kind of commotion?"

"Just a lot of cars."

"Do you see them?"

"No . . ."

"Wait a second, wait a second," Joy shouted. "Ozzy, cut a left!"

Ozzy shouted, "Are you crazy? We're over an embankment! There isn't even a road—"

"Cut a freaking left!" Joy screamed as the sirens drew nearer.

"Just do it!" I cried.

Ozzy spun the wheel and for the second time, the car began to bump and screech as it catapulted down the hillside, landing on hard-packed ground. He galloped through a field of pale green and yellow grasses that had probably been scenic before the car had torn through it. We kept going and going and going and going even after the sirens had begun to fade into the background.

One mile . . . two miles . . . three miles . . . until we all saw smoke come out of the hood of the car.

"Anyone see us go down?" I asked.

"Doesn't look like it," Zeke said. "Or maybe that's wishful thinking."

Ozzy slowed to a more acceptable speed. "Where are we?"

"I don't know the exact location," Joy said, "but I do know I used to ditch school back here with Antoine. He'd pick me up and we'd drive down here and hang out. If you . . ." She paused to catch her breath. "If you keep going toward that hill, then swing a right, there's an outlet to Crocheton Highway."

"Who's Antoine?" Zeke asked.

236

For God's sake, now's not the time for jealousy.

Another mile, another two miles . . . then three. We found the outlet to the highway.

"Think it's wise to get back on the highway?" Zeke asked.

"It's a different highway." Ozzy swung the police car back onto paved asphalt, causing a car to swerve around. I'm sure the driver would have cussed at us kids, but we were in a police car.

Even I knew where we were.

"In about six miles, we should hit the off-ramp for Buchanan," I told Ozzy.

He was in disbelief. "We might actually get out of this."

"Who's Antoine, Joy?" Zeke asked again.

"Six miles?" Ozzy frowned. "This car is red hot and so are we. We need to ditch it and the sooner the better."

All agreed. "Let's get off at the first exit," I suggested. "We can catch a bus."

Ozzy gave me a terse nod.

The traffic slowed us down and we were forced to follow the pace of the other cars around us. Obeying the rules was a skill that had escaped us for the past days. I didn't know why we were starting now. I put on the cop car's siren.

"Why'd you do that?" Ozzy said. "It'll bring attention to us."

"Drive on the shoulder," I told him. "Let's get out of here!"

"Good point, Hutchenson," Ozzy said.

We got off the highway and started looking for the correctly numbered bus stop. Joy told Ozzy that it was the number six bus that would stop a mile from Buchanan High.

"Thanks for ditching school, Joy," I told her.

"With Antoine," Zeke mumbled, "whoever he may be."

"Antoine's my cousin," Joy answered flatly.

"Kaida?" Ozzy said quietly.

"What?" I whispered.

"I can't come back with you."

I opened my mouth to speak, but nothing came out.

Ozzy stayed quiet. What could he say? *Psyche! Just kidding—I gotcha, Kaida!*

"What do you mean you can't come back?" I said.

"Bus is on the next block," Joy reminded us.

"I mean"—his fingers gripped the wheel—"I mean just that."

"Why not?" I asked.

"Marital dispute?" Zeke called from the backseat.

"Because I can't. . . . As much as I want to, I can't. I can't leave my mother. I can't leave my world. You have to leave, but I have to stay."

Tears welled up in my eyes. "Ozzy, you're a wanted man now! Escaping with us is your only chance to get away from the authorities."

"I know that. And I know if I stay I'm going to have to go underground. So will Maurice when the authorities find out about the forged papers." He took my hand and squeezed

238

it. "But if I find Maurice . . . maybe he can help us. Because he comes from where you come from. Kaida, someone has to stay in this world and *fight* this battle! If I leave . . . I take away everything that I've learned with me. And where will that leave everyone here?"

"But . . ." I didn't finish my sentence. What could I honestly say to that?

"I have to go back and check on my mom. I can't desert her like this." Ozzy pulled the car over to the curb and we all hopped out and started running to the bus stop. A few moments later, we were sitting on a graffiti-covered bench waiting with a few women with children to catch the bus.

"I'm not coming with you guys," Ozzy announced.

"You're kidding," Zeke said. "Why not?" He looked at me, and I shrugged.

I was far from home in this world. And now the only person who had made this world anything was leaving me.

Ozzy said, "Kaida, once you get back—"

"If I get back."

"You'll get back, Kaida. I know you will. And when you do, maybe we can communicate . . . your world to mine." His eyes were gleaming with wetness. "If anyone can bridge the gap, it'll be you. Together we can save a lot of people."

"What if the gap can't be bridged? What if 'bye' means 'bye'?"

His eyelids fell in a long blink. "Then at least I met someone who cared about life and love as much as I do."

I rested my head against Ozzy's chest as he stroked my hair and tucked it behind my ear. I wanted to stay that way forever. When the bus finally pulled up, all I saw was something big and ugly and evil, and I wanted to hit everyone on it. When we were finally seated, I felt my anger rise.

"You're going to forget about me," I told him. "This sucks!"

He cupped his hands around my face. "Okay, first of all, let's get a few things straight. You're leaving me—I'm not leaving you. Second of all"—he kissed my cheek—"I would never, ever forget you."

I wanted to say, *You don't know that.* I didn't know that. I wondered what would happen to me in this world when I left for my old world. And did I still exist in my old world now that I was in this new world? Everything that I had considered permanent, everything that had been a staple in my life—my family, my friends, my home—did they even exist anymore?

I put my head on his shoulder, closing my eyes and trying to live in the moment because that was all I had. Back in jail I wasn't sure that I'd ever taste freedom again, but we had each other. Here we were momentarily free, but I was going to lose him. Why does everything good have to be tainted with something bad?

He kissed my nose. "Don't worry about me. The past few days have shown me that there was a reason I tried out

Buchanan. That reason was to meet you and prepare me for this new life. We're going to win, Kaida. Maybe one day you'll come back and help us."

I sat up. "Iona Boyd! You have to be careful around her."

"What are you talking about?"

"Maurice said she's in with the government. That she's doing research just to provide the higher-ups with illegal medicine."

He was momentarily stunned. "All right. If I find Maurice, I'll ask him about her." He digested what I had said. "Thanks."

"And you'll be cautious?"

"It's my middle name . . . sometimes." He grinned. "No more talk, Kaida. Let's just be!"

There were thousands of things I wanted to tell him but I was just too tired.

Zeke checked his watch. "It's eight thirty, guys. We've only got a half hour until roll call."

"How far are we from the school?" I asked Joy.

"About two miles," she answered. "Our stop is next. It's about a mile away from school."

Zeke said, "We'll have to run it."

"Can Joy run?" I asked him.

"What choice do I have?"

"Next exit, we're out of here," Zeke said.

Ozzy took my hand. "Ready to go to school?"

"I'm ill-prepared on a regular day. How could I be ready on a day like this?"

Even if I were ready for school, I wasn't ready to leave Ozzy, willingly go on a field trip involving a car crash, a fire, a storm, a cave, and this time possibly death.

Finally the bus jolted to our stop and the doors opened. We were running as soon as our feet hit the ground.

We made it by five of nine.

Outside, my classmates were in a group talking, fooling around, sending text messages, or just sitting on the school's steps, half asleep.

"Kaida Hutchenson?" Mr. Addison called. "Kaida Hutchenson?"

I ran toward him and tripped, completely disoriented as to where I was. Emotionally I was a wreck. I looked up and found a hand extending toward me.

Sweet Ozzy . . . pulling me up. But instead of dark green eyes looking at me, the orbs were bright blue.

Zeke let go of my hand. "Are you all right?"

Ozzy? I looked around in a panic. "Where's Ozzy?"

"He left, Kaida."

"He was just here!" When I got no response, I said, "He came off the bus with us."

"He left when you started running to Mr. Addison."

I shook my head, too tired to cry. Not quite surprised enough to cry. I had been given fair warning.

Zeke put an awkward arm around me. "Hey, we have a

long car ride to exchange various shocking details."

I lowered my head on Zeke's chest, trying to dull a stinging inside my heart. He put both his arms around me and hugged me.

There it was.

Friendship at its oddest. And its finest.

21

Zeke and I pulled apart when Joy approached us. She looked exhausted, but she was smiling. "I guess I should bum one last smoke before we're transported back."

Zeke rolled his eyes. "Go for it."

"How's your arm?" I asked her.

She winced. "Not so good, but I think the Advil helped."

"Don't say the A-word so loudly," I reminded her.

She gave me a knowing nod. For the first time in a while I realized how putrid all of us smelled. "We really need to get back."

"Hey, guys," Mr. Addison greeted us. His ability to control

the students had dropped as time wore on. "We're . . ." He paused and wrote on his clipboard. "You three are with me."

"Yep!" Zeke said.

"You know that?"

We looked at one another and smiled. "Sort of."

"And, you're all okay with that?" Mr. Addison raised an eyebrow.

"Thrilled," Joy responded.

"Nothing sassy to say about it, Ms. Hutchenson?"

"Not at the moment." I looked over to my right and saw Maria waving to me as she slipped into Mrs. Dufraine's van. I waved back.

Mr. Addison tapped a pen against his clipboard. "Then let's load up."

We looked at him blankly. None of us had bags.

Mr. Addison said, "Your parents dropped off the bags this morning . . . all except Kaida's. We have to pick your stuff up at the house. Let's move it."

Again the three of us exchanged glances.

"Do we have a hearing problem ?" Mr. Addison said, "Let's get going."

Zeke got his bag and I helped Joy with hers. We loaded the van and belted up in the backseat, the three of us holding hands as Mr. Addison sped off to my house.

It seemed that no one was at home. Mom and Dad were at work and Suzanne was at day care. I didn't have my key so I used the spare one, hidden under the porch chair. As soon as I was in the house and the front door had closed, to my surprise Jace came down the stairs wearing pajama bottoms and a gray T-shirt.

"What are you doing home?"

"I packed your bags," he told me.

"Thanks, but why are you here and not at school?"

"I'm here . . ." Jace smiled at me. Bags had formed under his eyes. "To say good-bye."

"It's only a class trip."

"Kaida . . ." His eyes locked with mine. "I know what's going to happen."

I stared at him. "How?" When he didn't answer, I said, "Erin White?"

He thought a moment, then nodded. "You'll be here in body, you won't disappear, but it won't be the same you. All the knowledge that you brought with you from that world . . . it'll go back with you. Just like Erin's still here . . . but it's not the same Erin. Not the same at all."

"So where is your Erin?"

"I don't know for sure . . . but if you find Erin in your world, tell her I miss her."

"Is that where she is? In my world?"

"I sure as hell hope so. Because the Erin that exists now isn't the Erin I grew to love." He hugged me. "Just like you. I'll certainly miss you . . . the way you are now. And I won't forget you . . . ever."

I erupted into tears.

Jace smiled, but it was a sad one. "You were given this gift. You and Zeke and Joy . . . you were given this gift for a reason."

"What reason?"

"That remains to be seen." He hugged me tightly then twisted my earlobe. "You have to go, Kaida. Your bags are in your room."

My room . . . I reluctantly began the climb and Jace followed me. When I opened the door to my room, it looked the same as ever. The same white floor tiles, the same posters, the same mess. And the same photograph of the family with a newborn Suzanne outside my grandmother's house. When I went back, would the photo change back, too?

"Check your bags," he told me. "Make sure I didn't forget anything."

I frantically pawed through my stuff—sweatpants, sweatshirts, a jacket, underwear, power bars, canteen, water. "Flashlight . . . where's my—?"

Jace handed it to me and enveloped me in a hug.

"Kaida." He choked. "Take care of yourself. Please, please be careful."

"I will." I gasped for breath in his grip. Ordinarily I'd find it suffocating, but now it was nothing short of lovely.

"I love you," I told him.

"I love you, too." He pushed me away. "Go."

"Why didn't Mom or Dad phone school?" I asked suddenly.

"When I went missing, I mean?"

"I covered for you." Jace finally told me. "I covered for you, for Zeke, and for Joy. Because I *know*."

I thought a moment and got excited. "Maybe you can come with me."

He twisted my earlobe. "And maybe you can come back here." He gave me a mock stern look. "Go home, Lobeless."

"So, it was you and Ozzy?" Zeke nudged me. I was on his left; Joy was on his right weaving in and out of sleep as we traveled through the New Mexico desert.

"It was me and Ozzy," I confirmed. "Which is no longer an option." I smiled at him. "You and Joy?"

Zeke nodded, but his crystal blue eyes seem conflicted. "I wonder if back home, Leslie and I will be broken up or—"

"Eek!" I interrupted. "Someone has gotten himself into a lot of trouble."

"You bring up a good point, though." Joy spoke with her eyes closed. Her head was resting against Zeke. "When we get back, how altered will our lives be?"

"Assuming we get back," I added. "You know . . . add a dose of pessimism."

"More like fatalism," Zeke said. "If we don't get back, we might . . . we could be . . . you know."

The word was *dead*. But during ten days, its taboo status had rubbed off on us, and no one said anything.

"Maybe there will be an Ozzy when we get back," Zeke said matter-of-factly.

"I'm sure there will be an Ozzy," I told him. "But it won't be the same Ozzy. More than likely that Ozzy will have tried out Buchanan and left the school before I get back."

"How do you know?"

"I don't know, Zeke. I'm just . . ." I shook my head.

"Well, this might cheer you up." Zeke stuck his hand in his sweater pocket. "Ozzy told me to give something to you . . . if I can find it."

"What!" I exclaimed.

"Keep it down," Mr. Addison chided.

"Ozzy said to give it to you once we were far away." Zeke removed a piece of crumpled stationery with his right hand while stroking Joy's hair with his left.

"Hmmm," Joy purred. "Feels good."

"Why'd you wait so long?" I scolded him while whispering.

"Just following orders."

I plucked the paper from Zeke's grip, shaking.

"What does it say?" Joy asked.

"I don't know . . . I haven't read it." As I unfolded it, I turned toward the window for privacy. A note from my boyfriend . . . only he wasn't a boyfriend and I wasn't his girlfriend anymore.

Gah!

The paper was pale pink and lined with flowers, and it smelled like the knockoff perfume Dad had once bought Mom for her birthday. I unfolded it several times until it revealed the words that Ozzy had somehow found the time to write behind my back.

Then I realized he must have written it a few days ago. Probably all along he realized that he couldn't go back. He had his battles to fight.

Dear Kaida,
Well, I guess you're wondering where I got the stationery.

That wasn't utmost on my mind, but . . .

It's actually my mother's, so I'm giving you a part of me with it. You're probably thinking this is really a cheesy cop-out way to say 'bye' and you're probably not too happy with me right now. What can I say? You are the one who's gifted with remarkable powers. Use them wisely and maybe someday we'll be together again.

I just want you to know that I will never forget you—ever. Everything you've ever told me is etched inside my brain. Kaida, I need to stay behind. Not only do I have so much unfinished work here, I don't think the portal, so to speak, that will take you back will be able to take me back, because I never entered through it. Maybe that's a cop-out as well. Maybe someday I'll be brave enough to chance it and I'll meet you on the other side of the prism.

I wanted to be mad at him, but I couldn't. My eyes returned to the note.

I'm sorry I left without saying good-bye. But I've said good-bye to too many people I love and it hurt too much. Somehow we will find a way to stay connected.

Please don't forget me.

I'm going to draw you some doodles now.

Love,

Ozzy

I sighed.

"What does it say?" Zeke asked.

I turned around. "Sweet nothings." I tried to laugh, but my voice couldn't lie. "Nothing much."

"He really did like you, Kaida," Joy told me. "It was clear from the get-go."

Zeke nodded. "Why would he have bothered to help us if

251

he knew he wasn't coming back with us?"

"To get a link between our world and his," I answered without thinking.

"Oh-kay," Zeke said. "You're right. He risked helping us to get medicine for Joy just to get a way back to our world . . . which may be nonexistent."

When he put it that way, it did sound like I was trying to deny the obvious. He risked his life to help us. He risked his life because he liked me—and I would have done the same for him in a heartbeat.

I scratched my right ear. A piercing seemed to be getting infected.

All the more reason to be going home, I thought.

I put my head against the window, gradually succumbing to the rhythm of the van.

Sleep.

A warm sleep.

Warm . . .

Screeeeech.

Sweeeerve.

BOOM!

The sound was so deafening, I couldn't think, let alone hear.

Directly into my ear. Someone screaming.

"*Kaida!*"

I snapped open my eyes and Joy was hovering above me. "*Kaida, get out!*"

My eyes flitted across the scene. *Reds, oranges, yellows. Warm colors.*

"*Oh, my God!*" I cried. "It's happening, it's happening again!"

"Hold still!" Joy shouted over the crackling of flames.

"Why are you on top of me?" I choked.

"I'm trying to undo your seat belt!"

I looked down and saw that Joy's hands were black, attempting to unbuckle me. Without thinking I had accidentally clicked the buckle back onto myself, heat so fierce, it had turned to an icy feeling on my hands.

"Zeke!" Joy coughed. "Are you there?"

I could barely see through the smoke. Our world, aflame.

I sprung out of my seat and tried to find a way out of the van, but it seemed to be hot everywhere, worse than the last crash. How had I slept through the crash that long?

"Joy, Kaida!" Zeke called back. "Where are you?"

I desperately groped around for a way out, trying to feel for cold air that would mean fresh air and an opening. I would not have hands after this, I was sure of it.

"I can't get out!" Zeke screamed.

I couldn't see anything, but I felt a blazing metal handle. I said a three-second prayer and pulled.

The handle came off.

Still trapped, I lunged forward and touched a glass surface in front of me. Without warning, it shattered. I could make out the darker colors, blues and blacks outside. I charged forward, the heat surrounding me swiftly dissolving into the chill of the night. I knew I had scratched myself, but I didn't care. I ran like my feet were on fire—and they very well could have been. I couldn't stop running. I just continued on and on.

"Kaida!" a hoarse voice yelled. "Kaida, stop, stop running!"

"Stop!" another voice followed.

But I couldn't stop.

I heard footsteps quicken behind me and someone pulled me from behind, forcing me to stop.

"Kaida," Zeke gasped and gasped. "It's okay, you can stop."

I breathed heavily.

At this moment I became aware that Zeke's arms were wrapped around me in such a way that I could barely breathe. I looked down at my throbbing hand. It was black in some places from the smoke, but blistered red in other areas from the heat.

"I'm okay," I choked. "Zeke, let go of me."

"Right." Zeke let go and the two of us broke into coughing fits.

"Joy," I said in between coughs.

"She's"—*cough, cough*—"coming." Cough again. "I ran ahead to"—pant, pant—"stop you from running."

I looked around. The car was ablaze, looking like a sacrificial altar. We were at least five hundred feet from the explosion. From the distant light, I could make out Joy limping toward us.

"Hey," she said when she finally caught up to us.

Then, of course, she coughed. We hacked and wheezed like old men and women for about three minutes.

I finally said, "What about Mr. Addison?"

"I don't know," Joy told me.

"But we made it," Zeke said.

I nodded. Our eyes zeroed in on the three-story bonfire that once was the van. It was unlikely that Mr. Addison had survived. But this time the vehicle was already on fire before we got out.

"It didn't happen exactly like before," I said, still coughing. It was a gargantuan effort just to speak. My throat was rubbed raw. "Mr. Addison could be on the other side."

"Should we check?" Joy asked.

But then the sky opened up.

A downpour that within seconds turned torrential.

Last time we had cried when it had begun to rain. This time we nearly wept in ecstasy. It had never felt so good to have a serious case of déjà vu.

"There's the cave," Joy said breathlessly.

Outlined by the fire, Joy was pointing to a group of rocks that looked wonderfully familiar.

Zeke did a jig. "We're going home, we're going home!"

We began to laugh. Zeke attempted to do a pirouette and slipped on his own foot.

"Shit!" he cried, landing in the mud.

Joy extended her good arm to help him up, but she

slipped too. Zeke tried to get up, but he kept slipping further away, taking Joy with him.

"Here, grab my hand!" I screamed as I extended my hand toward them.

I think one of them tried to take it, but they both fell backward.

"Damn it!" Zeke said.

"No!" Joy shrieked.

"Wha—" I yelled.

"NO!"

"NOOOOOO!"

The blazing van, once our only source of light, was sizzling into smoke and blackness because of the rain. Everything around me became dark and slick.

"Guys?" I shouted desperately. I could barely see anything at this point. "*Guys!*"

I felt around.

No one was responding. I looked and looked and groped and groped, but I was utterly alone.

"No," I said to myself, "NO!"

What if they had fallen into the wrong portal? What if the correct portal to our world was still in the cave? What if they were in some other alternate universe: one where food or people didn't exist?

Or what if they had just fallen down a pit and died?

My face fell into my hands and I wept bitterly, getting drenched in the flood of water cascading from the sky. Out of exhaustion, I sat down and let the rain wash over me.

To steady my balance, I placed my hands on the ground, down into the mud, letting the ooze squeeze through my fingers, feeling the coolness of the slime quiet my burning hands.

Without a thought to pain, I pounded the ground.

Pounded it.

Pounded it and pounded it and *pounded* it until the ground opened up. I could feel the edge of a deep hole.

Knowing that it was up to me, that I was an inch away from falling into that abyss.

I traced the opening of the pit with my fingers, stuck my hand in, and felt nothing. No rain falling down, no walls, no barriers. Just something that was nothing.

Emptiness.

A space.

A void.

I dried my tears although it was a stupid thing to do. I was completely sodden from head to toe.

"Well," I said aloud, dangling my legs over the pit's opening. "Here's hoping for a world without math homework."

And with that, I slid my body forward with anticipation and dread.

My body plunging down.

Traveling to somewhere.

Flying through space and through the unknown.

257

22

"... yes ... a few second-degree burns, some gashes and cuts, and a minor concussion. They all escaped exceptionally well."

"So she'll be fine?"

"Given enough time, I'd say yes." A female voice. "Her hands are going to be bandaged for a while to protect them against infection. There may be a little scarring and blistering from the burns, but it's not her face, Mrs. Hutchenson. I assure all of you that—"

"Don't assure her of anything! The school assured us our children would be safe, and they've ended up in the ICU of some remote hospital in Timbuktu!"

"El Corazon, Mr. Anderson. And we're taking very good care—"

"Yeah, yeah, yeah!"

My eyelids slowly lifted. I wanted to ask, "Where's El Corazon?" but what came out was, "Eh eh Coz?"

"Kaida!" I heard Jace shout. "Mom, she's up!"

"Oh, dear Lord!" she exclaimed. My vision blurred and refocused, and I could see my mother. Another woman was glaring at a woman in pink scrubs.

"Oh, Kaida, sweetheart, can you hear me?" my mother pleaded, catching my weary eye.

"I told you she would wake up once the anesthesia wore off," the woman in pink scrubs preached.

"Great, lady. Can you give us a little privacy, please," a commanding man in black slacks ordered the pink-scrubs lady.

"Kaida," my mother said. "Can you see me? Can you hear me?"

I looked around.

ICU.

Someone had said ICU.

Intensive Care Unit.

Hospital?

"Thank God," I croaked aloud.

The room filled with muted laughter. "Thank God is right, dear." A soft-looking woman in sweatpants gave out a nervous chuckle. Atop her head was a messy gray bun.

"Zekenjoy?" I tried to ask. "Wheh ah Zekenjoy?"

My mother laughed out loud. "They're on either side of you."

Slowly my brain began to awaken from a very deep sleep.

The upside was that I could see.

The downside was my hands felt like they were on fire.

I realized I was in a very small room with a lot of people. Besides my parents, there were Jace; Mr. Warwick, the principal of my school; my math teacher, Mrs. Quentin; and another adult couple—the commanding man in slacks and his distraught wife. (I assumed it was his wife. She was definitely distraught.) Not to mention the woman with the messy gray bun and the pink-scrubs woman whom I figured to be a nurse.

". . . and another van, driven by Mrs. Quentin here, passed them and saw the fire."

Mr. Warwick was talking to the nurse.

"Mr. Addison," I said.

It came out "Mesah Addis . . ."

"Mr. Addison?" My mother's eyes became wet. "He's undergoing surgery for second- and third-degree burns."

I felt tears in my own eyes. Some of them were from sadness, but others were from happiness.

He *made* it.

Mr. Warwick kept talking. I wished he'd shut up, but then I realized that he sounded just as anxious as my parents.

"Thank God the kids seem okay."

"Thank God," the nurse repeated.

The principal's face loomed over mine. "Kaida, how are you feeling?"

"Quite chipper, I'm sure," Jace retorted.

I smiled inwardly. It was wonderful to see my Jace even if he wasn't the exact Jace I left. I wondered where Suzanne was and then realized that babies were not allowed in a hospital.

A hospital! What a wonderful word!

Mr. Warwick blinked. "If there's anything we can do—"

"I think giving her a bit of peace and quiet would be number one on the agenda," my father snapped.

"Who're . . . other people?" my strained voice tried. I wanted to make sure who I was seeing.

"The people?" My mother asked. "Zeke's parents, Joy's mother, and Mrs. Quentin, your math teacher. She saw the accident and picked you up in the rain." My mother's voice broke. "Do you remember the accident?"

Did I ever.

"Bits . . . " I fibbed.

"Nargh," I heard Joy sputter, waking up from her drugged-out state.

"Praise Mother Earth!" the lady with the bun said. I wondered for a second if she was a pagan.

I reached down to zip up my sweatshirt, feeling cold. Then

I realized that my hands were bandaged and I was in a hospital gown.

"Where . . . clothes?" I asked.

"I think they threw them out, honey," my father told me.

"No!" I cried. "No . . . my clothes."

"We'll buy you new ones," Mom said.

"No . . . my sweat . . . !"

"Your clothes—or what's left of them—are actually in a plastic bag in the closet down the hall," the nurse said. "They're full of ashes and mud."

"My sweat . . . sweatshirt!"

"Do you want them, Kaida?" Jace asked me.

I nodded as vigorously as I could, although I knew there was no way it had survived the blaze.

The nurse left the room and came back bearing a large plastic bag. I reached to take it from her but realized once again that my hands were completely bandaged.

"What would you like from it?" My mother grabbed the bag from the nurse.

"My sweatshirt."

"What?"

I thought I was talking clearly, but no one else did. "My sweatshirt," I tried again. "The pockets."

It was worth a shot.

Mom took out the sweater and turned each side of the center pocket inside out. A charred piece of paper drifted out as delicate as a fairy.

"The paper . . ." I mumbled. "Show me the paper."

Dad bent down and picked up the paper, glancing at it.

"Don't read it!" I hoarsely protested.

"Sorry!" My father held the piece of paper in front of my face. "Can you read it?"

I nodded.

Most of the note had been charred or burned away. But I could make out a few words and phrases, written in boyish handwriting.

Kaida, stationery, my mother's, gifted with remarkable powers, prism, stay connected, don't forget me.

Love,

Ozzy.

I felt myself grinning from ear to ear.

"Can I throw it out?" Dad asked.

I shook my head *no*!

"I'll keep it for you, Kaida," Jace told me.

I nodded.

My father's eyes were brimming over with tears. "You're incredibly lucky . . . and we're lucky because you're lucky!" He blinked, and wet tracks leaked across his cheeks. "Good Lord!" He walked away, covering his face in his hands.

"I'll go see if he needs anything," Jace said to my mother. He left the room.

"How long . . ." I asked my mother.

"What, honey?"

"How . . . long?" I said again.

263

"How long are you staying in the hospital?"

I nodded.

My mother kissed my forehead, dripping fat tears on my face. "As long as it takes for you to heal."